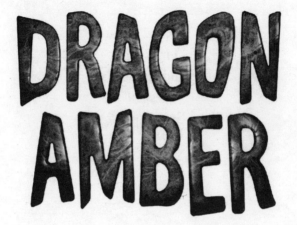

DRAGON AMBER

Books by C. J. Busby

The Amber series
Deep Amber
Dragon Amber

The Spell series
Frogspell
Cauldron Spells
Icespell
Swordspell

DRAGON AMBER

C. J. Busby

templar

A TEMPLAR BOOK

First published in the UK in 2014 by Templar Publishing,
an imprint of The Templar Company Limited,
Northburgh House, 10 Northburgh St, London EC1V 0AT
www.templarco.co.uk

1 3 5 7 9 10 8 6 4 2

ISBN 978-1-78370-057-8

Printed and bound in Great Britain by Clays Ltd, St Ives plc

For Celi, with love

Prologue

In the beginning was nothing but ice and darkness. Then a small crack appeared in the ice, and light flowed from it like a river. From the crack the World Tree grew, and as it grew it gathered warmth and life around it. The first humans and the first tree folk appeared, and they sheltered under the World Tree, and lived in the forest around it, and this land became the kingdom. As the Tree grew tall, new worlds grew like fruit from its spreading branches, and many travelled to live in those worlds.

But there were some creatures who preferred the ice and dark. The wolves, the crows, the dwarves and other dark creatures grew angry as their realm was everywhere pushed back, and they wanted to destroy the Tree and the worlds of light. So the forest folk – the tree guardians and those with magic – gathered *against the forces of the dark and became protectors of the Tree and the worlds it sheltered, and through all the generations since they have fought the dark wherever it tried to gain a foothold.*

But there was a time when the forces of ice and darkness grew increasingly powerful, and the kingdom could hardly hold them. The king, Bruni the One-eyed, was betrayed by his half-brother, Lukos, who was part human, part wolf, and a shape-shifter. He joined the creatures of darkness and used their magic to become even more powerful: the Lord of Wolves, immortal, impossible to kill. He fought hard against the kingdom and the worlds of light, until eventually it seemed they might lose the battle.

Then Bruni forged a sword of magical power, and he made four shallow cuts in the Tree. Tears of sap fell from the cuts and became bright, hard jewels of deep amber: one for the north, with flecks of brown earth; one for the south, with fiery flames at its heart; one for the west, with the power of the sea in its depths; and one for the east, the sky amber with the power of air. Each had the Tree's power over time and space and worlds. Then Bruni forged a crown out of Old Iron, and set the four jewels into it, and with the power of this crown he defeated the Lord of

Wolves and imprisoned him forever in a place made from slivers of every world and every time.

But the crown was a dangerous thing – just as it had the power to save the worlds, it also had the power to destroy them, and it could not be allowed to stay whole. When the battle was done, the king took his sword and cut the four pieces of amber out of the crown, and gave one to each of his four heirs. The eldest son kept the sky amber of the east and stayed to rule the kingdom after his father's death. The second son took the sea amber of the west into a world of water, and ruled this and nearby worlds, while the king's daughter took the fiery amber to the worlds of the south. The youngest son stayed in the northern world of cold iron. He took the earth amber as well as his father's sword, vowing to rid that world and those around it of the last remnants of the creatures of the dark. And so he did; but over the years the kingdoms of the three youngest heirs fell into decay, and the amber stones became scattered and lost.

It is said that if the four pieces of deep amber were to be found, and the crown remade, then the Tree and all the worlds would once again be in the greatest danger.

PART ONE

Chapter One

Jem had his head stuck down the castle well. He had been hanging upside down for ten minutes, not moving, waiting for his eyes to adjust to the gloom. His friend, Sol the butcher's boy, was keeping watch, but it was late afternoon and most of the castle was busy elsewhere. Gradually Jem began to make out details further down the well, where the neat, well-cut stones gave way to rougher-hewn stones covered with dark patches of moss. And then he saw it! A shadowy round hole – the entrance to what looked like a small tunnel leading from the side of the well towards the main castle. He pulled his head out and gazed at his friend in astonishment.

"You were right! I saw it! But how come

I never knew about this before? How come you never *told* me?"

Sol grinned, and shrugged. "I didn't know myself, did I? My grandad only showed it to me last week – when we needed somewhere really secret to hide the squire's undergarments. Somewhere even the dogs couldn't find them!"

Jem nodded in appreciation. It had been his idea originally, to steal the squire's undergarments and fly them from the battlements, but he hadn't been at Roland Castle when the plan was carried out. He'd been in another world – one without magic, but with all sorts of other interesting things. Custard creams and computer games and buses... Not that he could tell Sol that. The Druid had sworn him and Dora to secrecy about the whole thing – and you didn't break a promise to the Druid. He had quite a reputation for unusual and inventive punishments.

"Where does it go?" asked Jem, a speculative look on his face. It was time he announced his return to the castle with some notable act of mischief, or people would start to think he'd gone soft. This tunnel might be just what he'd been looking for...

"We didn't follow it all the way," said Sol. "It gets too small – you can't go more than a dozen steps. But Grandad said it goes to the castle cellar – there used to be some sort of pipe contraption that you could use to pump water down there, for potions and stuff."

"The cellar?" said Jem, his eyes brightening. "The Druid's cellar?"

"Yes," said Sol, puzzled. "But I told you – it gets really tiny. You can't get down it."

"That's what *you* think," said Jem, with a wicked grin. He pulled the well cover over and dusted his hands off.

"I'll see you at dinner," he said, nodding to Sol. "First I need to have a chat with Dora."

Dora was mucking out the pigs. It was her favourite job in the castle – no one disturbed you in the pigsties, and the pigs were always glad to see her. She was scratching Old Bessie on her back where she liked it, and fending off a few of the new piglets, when Jem vaulted over the stone wall and plonked himself down on the edge of the pig trough in front of her.

"I've found a secret way into the Druid's cellar," he announced with a flourish. "It leads from the old kitchen well. So I can sneak down there tonight – but you'll have to turn me small."

Dora looked at him in surprise. "Jem! Are you mad? Don't you remember what happened last time?"

The last time Dora had turned Jem small had been in the depths of the Great Forest, with a huge creature from another world stampeding towards him – and while Jem had survived the transformation, Dora had been quite unable to undo her own spell. It had been the queen's scheming nephew, Lord Ravenglass, who'd had to turn him back.

Jem grinned, and flicked his red hair out of his eyes cheerfully. "It's fine. I'm sure you'll manage to get it right, Dora. You won't have a – what was it? – an *elephant* charging straight at you when you do it this time!"

Dora sat down on an upturned bucket and considered. It was only a week since they'd returned from their adventures in the other world, but sometimes she found it hard to believe that it had been real. The strange 'swimming goggles' and 'camera' that had appeared in Roland Castle; meeting Simon, and his sister Cat, and finding the deep amber that had caused it all. She wondered how Simon and Cat were getting on, and whether Simon had worked out how to do any of the magic she'd shown him.

Dora glanced up at Jem. She probably could turn him small, she thought, and if she was concentrating when she did the spell, she was pretty sure she ought to be able to turn him back afterwards. If he really had found a tunnel to the Druid's workshop, then he could make sure he was hidden down there this evening when they knew that the Druid had an important meeting.

The Druid had been keeping Dora and Jem at arm's length ever since they'd returned from their adventures. When they asked what was happening, he just said he was "working on something" and that they "didn't need to know". But they were both determined not to be left out. They knew that there were four pieces of deep amber: Cat had one, and the queen, for now, had another. But that still left two pieces out there somewhere, and everything depended on getting to them before Lord Ravenglass. The Druid and the forest agents must be working on finding out where those bits of amber were.

And a bit of listening at doors and quizzing the chambermaids had revealed that the Druid was expecting a special visitor from the Great Forest to meet him that evening, in his workshop.

"OK," said Dora. "It's the only way we're going to find out what's going on. I'll do it."

Jem whooped. "I knew you'd agree. Come on – I'll help you finish the pigs and then we can sort out a plan!"

The small tunnel from the kitchen well was extremely dark, and the stones that lined it were slippery with moss. Jem, magicked down to the size of a dandelion, was on his hands and knees in the entrance, peering up at the greyish twilight at the top of the well.

"Are you all right?" called Dora softly. "Have you got down there yet?"

"Yes, I'm in!" called Jem. He could see Dora's silhouette against the grey sky, but couldn't make out anything of her expression. Not that he needed to, he thought. She would have a worried look in her brown eyes, and a small crease between her eyebrows. He grinned. "I'm fine!" he called. "Leave the rope hanging down so I can get out again – and go and find something to do for an hour or so. It'll be suspicious if you hang around the well all evening!"

Dora nodded. "Good luck!" she called, and watched as Jem activated the small magical werelight she'd given him and started to feel his way into the tunnel. Then she pulled the cover back over, leaving a small chink for Jem to crawl through when he got back. She tiptoed off to find something inconspicuous to do, crossing her fingers that Jem would get down the tunnel all right, and that he wouldn't encounter any rats.

By the time he got to the Druid's cellar Jem was cold, peckish and slightly regretting his offer to be turned small. He should have brought a jerkin and a hunk of bread or something, he thought. But at least he had made it all the way down the tunnel – and it *did* lead to the Druid's cellar. Sol's grandad had been right. The tunnel ended half way up the wall, just above an old water butt in the corner near the cellar stairs. There had been bits of old decayed pipework in the tunnel, but nothing Jem couldn't crawl round or over, and although there was a hinged wooden cover over the end of the tunnel, it was very rotten and there were plenty of holes Jem could peer through. He could see the tall, lanky figure of the Druid on the other side of the cellar, pottering around with bits of potions and writing occasional notes in the margins of a big, old spell book. Jem settled down and prepared to wait.

He didn't have to wait long. Almost as soon as he'd curled himself into the corner by the biggest hole, there was a rattle at the top of the stairs, and a breath of wind caused the candles in the cellar to gutter. A heavy tread could be heard on the steps, and then, with a slight grunt of breath, a rather rotund, balding man in blue overalls entered the cellar. Jem sat up eagerly. It was Albert Jemmet, the forest agent they'd met in Cat and Simon's world.

"Albert!" said the Druid, looking up from his books. "At last!"

"Yes, well, sorry about that," said the portly man, walking over to give the Druid a friendly thump on the back. "Bit of trouble with your castle gate guards. No chance of a mug of tea, I don't suppose?"

The Druid grinned and gestured at a nearby

armchair. On a small stool next to it stood a steaming mug and a bowl of sugar lumps.

"Ah – excellent!" said Albert, lowering himself into the chair and stirring six lumps of sugar into his tea with a sigh. He took a good slurp and then looked up, his expression business-like. "So. We've found one of them."

Jem stiffened. He could see the Druid's startled expression and Albert's nod of satisfaction. This was it! They'd found one of the missing pieces of amber! Jem craned forward to try to get a better look.

The Druid sat down opposite Albert and conjured a second mug of tea for himself.

"Where?" he said, taking a large gulp.

Albert's expression turned rather serious. "It's not good news, I'm afraid," he said. "All the indications are that it's in the Akkadian Empire."

The Druid spluttered tea down his front and choked. Albert had to give him a firm whack on the back.

"The Akkadian Empire?" he said faintly, when he had recovered. He ran his hands through his messy dark hair, looking appalled. "Are you sure?"

Albert nodded. "It looks like it. We can't be

sure where, exactly, and it doesn't seem to have been used for a very large number of years, but according to the research we've done, it's almost certainly still there. We think it's the southern amber, the fire amber."

"Dragon amber," mused the Druid, rubbing his chin. "It would fit."

Albert took a slurp of tea. "Of course, we haven't had an agent in that world for generations. Not officially."

"No," said the Druid slowly. "And it won't be easy to get anyone in there now. Any attempt to find the amber will have to be quick, and very secret. One agent only."

"Exactly," Albert said, and looked at the Druid with a very neutral expression in his blue eyes. "There was quite an argument in the forest about what to do, but it's finally been agreed. We want you to be the one who goes."

The Druid met his gaze, then nodded. "I rather thought you might," he said heavily. "But you know – I didn't get away very easily last time. They want my head."

Albert raised one eyebrow. "What exactly did you *do* last time?"

The Druid looked slightly shamefaced. "I – er – well. I stole a dragon. A royal one. As a matter of fact, she still lives here – in a cave up near Whitestone Peak."

Jem gasped. So that explained where the dragon had come from! The Druid had brought it from another world. No wonder he always looked a little guilty whenever the dragon or its offspring caused trouble – and no wonder they were the only castle in the kingdom that had real dragons! Jem shook his head, wonderingly. He'd always liked the dragon on Whitestone Peak – so much so that he'd tried to hatch a couple of the dragon's eggs himself when he'd found them abandoned by the millstream last autumn. The baby red dragons had caused no end of trouble when they'd got bigger, and the Druid had had to banish them from the castle – after giving Jem a very thick ear. But they still occasionally swooped down when he was out and about in the countryside and gave him a friendly peck on the ear. For some reason they seemed to think he was their mother.

Jem was so busy thinking about the dragons that he missed the next bit of conversation, but when he looked up again, Albert was offering the Druid a rather ornate painted tile.

"It's all we've got from that world," he was saying. "It'll get you into the temple, anyway, and it's pretty damn certain that the amber will be in the control of either the royal court or the priests."

The Druid shook his head. "Sorry, Albert. I'm not walking straight into that hornets' nest. I've got a memento of my own. It will do me fine."

He rummaged in a cupboard for a few minutes and then came up holding a small brass teapot, tall and elegant, with an intricately wrought handle.

"The Western bazaar," he said. "I should be able to find a few old friends there – keep a low profile, avoid any guards or officials…"

He looked across at Albert, his brown eyes troubled. "You know, I – ah – I might not make it back. You'd better be prepared to send someone else if…"

Albert nodded. "If we have to," he said. "But I'm hopeful. You're our best agent."

"Ex-agent," said the Druid, with a wry smile. He shrugged. "I think I'd better go straight away. We have no idea how close Ravenglass might be to finding it. And besides, if I wait too long, I might think better of it."

He pulled an old travelling pack off a hook on the wall, and slipped a small dagger into his belt. Then he held the teapot in front of him, and started to make a series of gestures over it, muttering some strange words. A white mist formed in front of him, and then took the shape of a doorway. The Druid glanced over at the stocky figure of Albert and gave him a thumbs up.

"Wish me luck!" he said, and stepped into the mist.

Albert sighed, as the mist popped out of existence.

"Good luck!" he said softly. He propped the ornate tile against one of the Druid's spell books and took a final gulp of his tea, before trudging slowly out of the cellar.

Jem realised he had been holding his breath. He let it out in a big whoosh, and started to crawl back up the tunnel. He had to get to Dora. He had to tell her what had happened. They could use the tile to follow the Druid, and help him find the amber.

Chapter Two

When Jem finally hauled himself out of the castle well, it was properly dark, with only a few stars visible between the clouds. The wall of the Great Tower loomed above the well, illuminated by the faint glow of a brazier from the battlements. Up on the ramparts, the castle guards were stamping their feet and complaining about the cold, their armour jingling faintly.

Dora was wrapped in her warmest cloak, sitting huddled and half asleep on a stone bench by the tower. Her eyes kept drifting shut, so it was a few minutes before she noticed Jem sitting on the well cover and waving his arms at her.

"Jem!" she called softly, as she hurried over. "What took you? You were ages!"

Jem grimaced. "Met a rat," he said.

"A rat!" said Dora. "Are you all right?"

He waved his short sword at her.

"Stuck it in the bum," he said with satisfaction. "It ran away. But I got a bit turned around after the fight – ended up going down a side tunnel. Took me ages to find the way back!"

There was a sudden noise from above them on the battlements, and then a burst of laughter. Dora hurriedly leant over to scoop Jem up.

"Come on," she said. "We'd better head back to my room before I turn you back, or someone will see us."

She slipped into the Great Tower and then down a series of long stone corridors before climbing to the turret room where she slept. Placing Jem on the floor, she raised her arms and said the words of the reversal spell.

Jem seemed to glow slightly. The next moment he was standing in front of her, a sturdy red-haired fourteen-year-old, exactly the right size. Dora sat down on her bed in a flood of relief. She had done it! She had been worried it would go wrong again and leave Jem tiny. Her spells must be getting more reliable, she thought, pleased.

Jem grinned appreciatively and flexed his arms.

"Well done, Dora! I think you might even have managed to make me a little bit taller!" He pulled her upright and stood next to her, measuring where the top of her head came to – just about level with the end of his rather long and slightly crooked nose.

"Yep!" he said cheerfully. "Definitely taller."

Dora rolled her eyes. "I doubt it very much," she said. "I didn't put any growing magic into the spell. Just a straight reversal. You look *exactly* the same size to me."

Jem shrugged. "Oh, well – maybe next time," he said with a grin. "But right now we have to make plans. The Druid's gone after one of the bits of amber – and I know where!"

Dora sat back down on the edge of her small bed and hugged her cloak round her. "He's gone?" she said. "On his own?"

Jem pulled a stool over and sat on it, facing her. His eyes were shining. "Yes. Albert Jemmet told him where it was – some empire or other – and then he just went. Albert had brought this bit of tile from that world, so the Druid could use it to get there. But the Druid had this funny jug he wanted to use instead. So Albert left the tile behind. Which means we can go after him! We can use the tile!"

Dora looked at Jem's eager expression and bit her lip. They had both agreed that they were not going to be left out – that whatever it took, they were going to help find the other bits of amber and make sure Lord Ravenglass didn't get there first. But Dora had imagined finding out what the Druid was up to and then confronting him – insisting he take them with him. She hadn't thought they might have to go to a strange world by themselves, knowing nothing about what might be on the other side of the portal. Dora had a feeling that they had got off lightly on the last occasion they'd come up against Lord Ravenglass and his allies. She wasn't desperately keen to be stuck in another world with Jem, not knowing exactly where the Druid might be, or who else might be hunting for the amber... But the amber had to be found, and the Druid was there on his own. The Druid was easily the strongest magic-user she had come across, but if the dark crow men, Smith and Jones, appeared, even he would find it hard to fight off both of them without help.

She swallowed.

"OK," she said at last. "You're right. We'll have to go after him. But we ought to get a good night's sleep first, and then see if we can find out anything about this world in the morning. The Druid's got loads of old books – one of them might have some useful information."

Jem shook his head in exasperation. "We should go *now*, Dora – every minute counts!"

"No," said Dora firmly. "We need some sleep. And we can gather supplies in the morning. We have no idea what's on the other side, Jem – and we'll be coming through in a different place to the Druid. It could take a while to find him. We need to be at least a little bit prepared!"

Jem looked mutinous, but then he nodded. Dora was probably right. They could make better preparations in the morning.

But in the end, they didn't get a chance to make any preparations at all. Because at dawn the castle was attacked by Lord Ravenglass's army.

Dora woke to the sound of shouting and the clash of swords. It was still dark, but when she looked up at the small window in her turret room she could see that the sky outside was pale grey. There was an odd, flickering orange glow reflecting off the stones at the edge of the window. Dora frowned at it, still half asleep. What was going on? And then she heard the shout from below: "Fire!"

Fire? Suddenly Dora felt very wide awake. She threw herself out of bed and pulled on her grey dress. As she knelt to fasten her boots, she heard feet pounding up the turret stairs and Jem burst into the room.

"Dora!" he gasped, bending over against the door to catch his breath. "It's Ravenglass's men. They marched up to the castle an hour ago, demanding entry. Sir Mortimer let them in, but then they started disarming the guards and insisting they were in charge now. Sir Roderick refused to give them his sword, and then it turned into an all-out fight. They've set the stables on fire!"

Dora ran to the window and craned her head out to see what was going on below. Jem was right, the stables were on fire, and she could hear the whinnying of terrified horses and people shouting as they tried to lead them away or douse the flames. In the orange glow she could see figures fighting hand to hand in the courtyard, but there was smoke everywhere and it was hard to make out who was who.

She turned to Jem. "How many men?" she asked urgently. She was doing a rapid head count of the castle knights. Many of them were old and not particularly quick on their feet. Of the younger, fitter knights there were probably only a handful, plus twenty-odd squires and the serving men, who might be good in a scrap but didn't have much to protect themselves against well-armed soldiers. If Lord Ravenglass's troops were more than about thirty men, the castle was as good as lost.

Jem's face was grim. "I didn't see them arrive – but Violet and Annabel raised the alarm. They were out collecting early morning dew or some nonsense like that. They said there were at least a hundred soldiers and about twenty knights."

Dora felt as if all the air had been sucked out of her. A *hundred* men? What was Lord Ravenglass thinking? She looked at Jem, and the answer came to them both in the same instant.

"The amber!"

"We've got to warn the Druid!" said Jem at once. "He mustn't come back here with it – or it will go straight to Ravenglass!"

Dora nodded and grabbed her cloak from the end of the bed. She looked round the room rapidly to see if there was anything else she ought to bring, but her brain wouldn't work. She had a nasty feeling there was something very, very important that she ought to be remembering to take, but all she could think of was the Druid stepping back through a portal to the cellar of Roland Castle and finding himself surrounded by Lord Ravenglass's men.

"Come on!" said Jem. "Quickly! If we head for the North Tower we can get straight down to the cellars without crossing the courtyard."

Dora hesitated, then followed him out of the door, wrapping her cloak around her as she went.

The smell of acrid smoke grew stronger as Dora started down the turret stairs. By the time they were feeling their way through the dark passageways above the courtyard, her eyes were stinging and the sound of shouts and the ringing of swords on armour was much louder. As they turned into a smaller corridor that went past the knights' chambers, one of the doors banged open and Sir Bedwyr stumbled out, looking wild-eyed. He was dressed in his undergarments, his large feet bare and his black hair sticking out in all directions, but his sword was in his hand.

"Dora!" he hissed. "Jem! What in the kingdom is going on?"

"S – Sir Bedwyr!" stuttered Dora, trying not to look at the handsome knight's state of undress. "We're under attack! Lord Ravenglass... But how did you not wake up before now?"

Sir Bedwyr looked embarrassed. "I – er – I may have overindulged last night... A few too many flagons of – well, never mind. But Lord Ravenglass? Why– ?"

Jem grabbed the knight urgently by the arm. "He wants the amber. The Druid's gone to get another piece of deep amber and somehow Lord Ravenglass has found out. We're going to try to warn him not to come back. But –" he glanced at Dora – "someone ought to warn the forest. Maybe...?"

Dora nodded, and turned to Sir Bedwyr.

"There are a hundred of Ravenglass's soldiers, and twenty knights. The castle won't hold out much longer. But we know Albert Jemmet left for the forest only last night – he'll have taken the Bridbury road. If you could get away – find a horse – you could catch up with him. Warn him!"

Sir Bedwyr ran his hands through his hair, making it stick up even more, and looked as if he was thinking hard. Then he nodded. "Warn Albert," he said. "Right. But I'm not exactly dressed for—" He gestured down at his bare feet, and rubbed his chin. As he did so, there was a resounding crash at the other end of the corridor and suddenly the sound of fighting was much, much nearer. The knight quickly pushed Jem and Dora behind him and drew himself up to his full height.

"Go!" he commanded. "I'll do what I can, and then I'll try to get off after Jemmet."

He advanced down the corridor, still in his undergarments.

"Sir Bedwyr!" he shouted as he gathered pace, holding his sword with a firm two-handed grip. "Sir Bedwyr for Roland Castle!"

He disappeared round the corner and the

sound of swords clashing on armour suddenly increased tenfold.

Dora winced at the thought of Sir Bedwyr's lack of chain mail, but Jem was pulling her further down the corridor.

"Come on!" he urged. "He'll be all right! He's the best fighter in the castle. But we need to get to the cellars while the way's still clear!"

The Druid's cellar was exactly as he had left it. The noise of fighting was barely audible this far underground, and so far none of the smoke had seeped down from the courtyard. Jem and Dora had had a couple of anxious moments reaching the doorway that led to the cellar stairs, but they had made it. Jem's leggings were singed, his face just a little bit sooty, but he was holding up the other-world tile in triumph.

"Here! This is it! A tile from the palace of the… something Empire. Akkandan or something like that."

Dora took the tile cautiously. It felt heavy, as if there was metal in it. When she looked closely, she could see the gleam of gold in the ornate, geometric pattern. Gold, and what looked like copper, as well as a brilliant deep-blue stone which shone at the centre of an eight-pointed star. She tried to sense something of the world it had come from, but it just felt cold, hard. There was magic there, she thought, but very controlled – kept in sharp, straight lines like the patterns of the tile itself.

She started to say the words of the portal spell, reaching out to find a connection between the cold hardness of the tile and the warm, magic feel of her own world. There! She felt the magic take hold – and a swirling white mist formed in front of her. She looked at Jem and he nodded. Warily, he loosened his short sword in its scabbard, and together the two of them stepped into the portal and disappeared.

PART TWO

Chapter Three

The first time Simon managed to magic a portal to the kingdom it was a complete disaster. He tried the spell at least fourteen times before he could conjure even a wisp of white mist, and by the time he'd firmed it up into a portal it was nearly time for Mum to arrive home from work. Even so, Simon was determined to at least stick his head through and see what was on the other side. But as he cautiously approached the white mist, something small and furry came hurtling out of it in the other direction and flew straight into Simon's face. He yelled, and flapped, and then overbalanced backwards, while the strange furry object started whizzing all round the room, knocking things flying and chirruping frantically. Finally, it dived down to where

Simon was sprawling, and started to burrow its way into a pile of discarded clothes on the floor.

Simon twisted round, grabbed his red hoodie and threw it swiftly over the creature. He could feel it struggling underneath the layer of cloth.

"Got you!" he said triumphantly. "I think you need to go back where you came from!"

But as he turned back to the portal there was a rattling, throaty sound, and out of the mist stalked something else. Something about the size of a large goose, but altogether more vicious. Simon barely had time to register its thin, scaly legs, sharp claws, pointed beak, and fiercely intelligent yellow eyes, before the creature was jabbing its beak into Simon's hands and face and tearing with its razor-sharp claws into the red hoodie he was holding.

"Help! Help! *Cat!*" yelled Simon, trying to elbow the creature away from his face and at the same time bundle the wriggling hoodie up under his body, out of the way of the vicious beak and claws. "*Catrin!*"

Simon's bedroom door crashed open and his older sister appeared in the doorway. Her eyes widened as she took in the scene of chaos in front of her.

"Simon! What the – ? What is that…? Oh my God – what have you *done*?"

"Ow! Cat! Get it *off* me, can't you?" yelled Simon, curling himself up into a ball while the creature continued to jab and claw at him, trying to get at the bundle underneath his body.

Cat hesitated, and then ran for the bathroom. She came back with a wooden toilet brush, which she held out in front of her as she inched towards the creature. It stopped jabbing Simon and looked up, cocking its head to one side and regarding her with one evil yellow eye. Just as it tensed to spring at her, Cat whacked it round the head with the toilet brush. The creature looked momentarily dazed, but then it screeched angrily and started to peck at her, while Cat retreated, getting in the odd jab with the toilet brush but being steadily beaten backwards.

"Simon – do something!" she shouted, as the creature lunged forward. Simon grabbed a heavy encyclopaedia from his floor and brought it down on the creature's head. The creature rolled over, out cold.

"Back through the portal!" gasped Simon "Before it wakes up!"

The creature's eyelids were already flickering. The two of them rapidly shoved its dead weight towards the misty doorway. The creature's claws were starting to flex now, but it was halfway into the mist, and after one last heave it disappeared. The portal closed behind it with a faint pop.

There was a moment of relieved silence as Cat and Simon looked at each other, breathing hard. Cat was thirteen, two years older than her brother, and she was supposed to be in charge on days like this, when Mum was away at a conference or museum workshop. She was supposed to be responsible, and Simon was supposed to do as he was told. Simon pushed his straight dark hair out of his brown eyes and looked at her with his best apologetic expression, but it was not enough to pacify her.

"Simon – you idiot! What were you *doing*? You opened a *portal*? *Without me*?!"

Simon dabbed at his forehead, where the creature had managed to land a jab with its sharp beak, and winced. He looked at the smear of blood on his fingers.

"Ouch..." he said. "Umm, yeah. Well, I know, I'm sorry. I should have told you. It's just – well – I wanted to see if I could do it. I wanted to practise first, before we did it together. In case I couldn't."

He bit his lip, lowered his gaze, and tried to look as if he was truly very, very sorry. Usually that was enough to bring out Cat's motherly side, and when Simon glanced over, he was expecting to see her look a little less stern. Cat, however, was still grim-faced, running her fingers through her short blonde hair and frowning. Simon touched his forehead again and showed her his fingers.

"Look! Blood..." he said in a wheedling voice. "Blood, Cat. You can't be mean to me. I'm *bleeding*!"

She tried to keep a straight face, but then the corner of her mouth twitched. She shook her head at him in mock exasperation.

"It would serve you right if you bled to death," she said. "I can't believe you did something so dangerous without me! And Mum's due back any minute! Your room's a total mess –"

"Well that's normal," put in Simon swiftly.

"But what if the creature had got free? What

would we have done if it had gone running off down the road? 'Oh, sorry, everyone, we let a dinosaur-thing from another world loose in Wemworthy!'"

Simon looked abashed. It was true, he shouldn't have done the portal magic without Cat. He'd just so wanted to impress her with his ability to get it right – to do magic, to conjure a portal first time.

It was only a week since Simon and his sister had first come into contact with magic, and learned that there were other worlds. Their dad, who had died in a car crash when Simon was three, had come from one of them – the kingdom. It was a world of castles and magic, knights and dragons. A world that had suddenly, mysteriously, become entwined with their own for a few short days.

A lot had happened in those days – they'd made new friends, new enemies; they'd learned about the power of deep amber to open rifts between worlds and close them again; and they'd prevented a piece of that amber being stolen by Lord Ravenglass, the regent of the kingdom. The amber itself was now safely round Cat's neck –

because it was Cat who had picked it up in the heat of the battle, and so it was Cat who was now the rightful owner. Both of them, it turned out, were heirs of the kingdom, both had magic, and either of them could have taken the amber – but it was Cat who had been closest.

Simon looked at the gleam of the bronze chain around Cat's neck. He was only just getting used to the idea that he had magical abilities, but he was determined to make the most of them. If he wasn't going to have the amber, he was going to make sure he had the strongest magic, and the best sword-fighting skills.

He reached out and picked up the shining broadsword that was lying in the middle of his carpet, running his fingers down the engravings along its length. Of all the strange and astonishing things that had happened to him over the last week, the thing that had meant the most to Simon had been finding the sword. The sword had belonged to his dad, Gwyn, and it was what Simon had been using to conjure the portal to the kingdom. Simon was full of curiosity about the kingdom, eager to see it for himself. But there was more to it than just wanting to go to the place where his dad had grown up. Even though he knew it was mad, there was a tiny part of him that hoped his dad hadn't really died in that car crash. Maybe, just maybe, he'd gone back there, to the kingdom. Maybe he was alive somewhere, trapped, unable to return.

It was Dora, from the kingdom herself, who had shown him how to make a portal. "You need an object from the world you want to go to," she'd whispered as they slipped behind a sofa while everyone else was talking. "Then you can use it to make a link to that world, the one the object came from." It was a complicated spell, but Simon had concentrated very hard. And even though his first attempt hadn't gone quite as he'd planned, at least he'd made a portal! He'd done magic!

Simon grinned up at Cat, and had just opened his mouth to say as much, when there was a loud chirruping sound, and Simon's hoodie, on the floor, started to bulge in a rather peculiar fashion.

"Simon!" said Cat, startled, and stepped backwards. Simon suddenly remembered the small furry creature that he had been protecting. It had got left behind! He gave Cat an apologetic look, and picked the hoodie gently off the floor.

Sitting on the carpet, looking up at them with two dark eyes, was something that resembled a brown furry ball. It chirruped, and then bounced onto Simon's lap and chirruped some more. Then it snuggled up into his jumper and started to make a tiny purring sound.

Cat raised her eyebrows.

"It came through the portal," said Simon, picking up the small creature and stroking it. It blinked at him and chirruped a couple of times, flapping two stubby, furry wings. Now it was closer, he could see that it had two short legs and delicate feet like a chick, but with its round head, fat body and deeply ruffled feathers it closely resembled a fluffy pom-pom. "That other – thing – was chasing it, and now it's got left behind. We'll have to look after it till we can take it back."

Cat rolled her eyes. "What are we going to tell Mum?" she said. "And where can we keep it? And what – oh!" She broke off as the creature, which had turned its head at the sound of her voice, flew over to her and snuggled onto her lap. Now it was looking up at her with its dark eyes and chirruping gently.

Cat put her hand out and stroked it, and it

started to make a throaty, purring sound. She smiled in delight and tickled it under the chin.

"See?" said Simon, "It's sweet. We should give it a name. And we can keep it in the old hamster cage – Mum'll never notice it's not a hamster. I'll say Jake at school gave me one of his."

Cat sighed. "OK. It is very sweet. And I daresay we can take it back with us eventually."

She pushed the creature off, onto the floor, and then lay on her stomach watching it preen itself and bob its head up and down at them both. Then she looked up at Simon, her expression serious.

"But if you ever do anything like this again – if you ever try to conjure a portal without me – I'll go straight to Mum and tell her everything. It's too dangerous! You could end up anywhere! Lord Ravenglass is out there somewhere – and so are those horrible crow men! Smith and Jones. If we're going to do anything, we do it together, OK?"

Simon nodded. He definitely didn't want to meet Lord Ravenglass. The thought of his elegant black ringlets and his lazy drawl made Simon shudder. And he could feel a cold finger tracing itself down his spine as he thought about the tall, thin men in black suits, Mr Smith and Mr Jones, with their shiny black eyes and their bird-like way of walking.

"OK," he said. "I promise. We'll stick together. Whatever happens."

Chapter Four

It was a few days before Simon and Cat got another chance to try portal magic. In the meantime, the small, furry ball from another world had started to make himself at home in the old hamster cage – although where he preferred to be, if possible, was in Simon's pocket or down the front of his jumper. Simon had named him Frizzle, and although Cat wasn't generally fond of animals, even she was coming round to the idea that they should let him stay.

"He'll only get eaten by one of those dinosaur things if we take him back," Simon argued. "He's much better off here, with us."

"He does seem quite happy," Cat agreed, stroking the top of his furry head while he purred noisily. "But I'm still not sure... Doesn't it cause some kind of imbalance – things being out of place like that?"

Simon frowned. "Albert said something like that, when all those objects got swapped between here and the kingdom. But it can't be too terrible or they wouldn't have let us keep the sword. And anyway – Dad and Uncle Lou and Great-Aunt Irene lived here for ages, and they're all from the kingdom originally."

Cat hesitated, then nodded. "OK, we'll let him stay. But we'd better check with Albert or Uncle Lou, when we see them next."

Simon tickled Frizzle under the chin. "Hear that, Frizzle? You can stay! Nice sunflower seeds and chocolate drops and no nasty dinosaur things!"

Frizzle chirruped, blinked his dark eyes and then flew to Simon's shoulder and burrowed down happily into the neck of his jumper.

"Right," said Cat briskly, clearing a space in the centre of Simon's bedroom. "To work! Mum's not back from the museum till six, and we've done all the weekend chores, so we've got hours. Let's explore a bit of the kingdom at last."

Simon pulled the sword out from under his

bed, and held it out in front of him. He glanced at Cat.

"Are you ready to deal with one of those creatures, if we get another coming through?"

Cat waved a large bath towel in front of her and flourished the wooden toilet brush, like a matador ready to deal with a charging bull.

"All set," she said cheerfully. "Breakables away, door shut, weapon at the ready."

Simon took a deep breath and tried to concentrate on the portal magic. It had taken ages to work out exactly how to access the magic inside him, even with Dora's help – a bit like trying to work out how to waggle your ears or flare your nostrils. Even after days of practice it still took a few moments to get the right bit of his brain working – but he could feel it now, beginning to bubble up inside him. He ran his fingers down the sword and started to say the words of the spell. Wisps of white mist began to form in front of them. Simon focused hard on the portal magic and the mist started to firm up. Then suddenly there it was: a white doorway, in the middle of the room.

He looked at Cat triumphantly and saw that

she had her mouth open. She shut it hurriedly. Then she took a firm grasp of the towel and started to walk forward.

"Stay this side," she said. "And keep hold of my jumper. We don't want it to close behind us till we've had a good look – checked there's nothing too nasty on the other side."

Simon nodded, and took hold of the back of Cat's jumper as she tentatively poked her head through the white mist. He could hear her voice, the other side, calling back to him, but it sounded a little as if she'd wrapped the bath towel round her head – muffled and far away.

"Uurgh! It's raining! And – it doesn't look like I thought it would." She stepped back into the bedroom. Her short blonde hair was plastered to her head and water was dripping down her nose. "It's like a swamp. With all these peculiar trees. No castles in sight."

"Here – let me look," said Simon, and pulled her out of the way. Cat started to rub her head vigorously with the bath towel.

"Be my guest," she said, gesturing at the portal.

Simon moved forward warily and stuck his head into the mist. There was a slight resistance, and then he was through, looking out on a whole different world. Cat was right – it was wet and swampy, and the trees were tall and sinuous, their branches flame-red with spiky purple leaves. There was a splash nearby, and Simon realised that what looked like swampy ground was actually some kind of green algae or pondweed covering an expanse of brown peaty water. Ripples ran out from where the splash had created a dark pool. Then, from the middle of the pool, a head emerged. A large head, a little like a crocodile's but covered in silvery scales. It had a wide mouth and alert, hungry red eyes. The eyes focused on Simon, and the creature held still, regarding him. Simon could see spines on the back of its head. *A dragon?* he thought. *Some kind of sea serpent?* Then the creature seemed to gather itself together, and the next moment it was shooting towards Simon like an express train, a vast expanse of silvery body emerging from the lake behind it.

"Aaarghh!" yelled Simon as he shot out of the portal. He threw himself backwards so fast that he fell over, sprawling on the floor of the bedroom and waving frantically at the misty doorway.

"Close it!' he shouted.

"What? *How?*" cried Cat, flapping her towel at the portal as a long scaly snout started to quest through the mist, nostrils flared, sharp, curved teeth visible in its mouth. "Simon! *How do you close it?*"

Simon couldn't think. Dora hadn't said anything about closing a portal – you just went through it. Once someone had gone through it, it seemed to just close on its own. Would throwing an object through have the same effect? The snout was further into the room now, weaving from side to side as the creature tried to work out what this strange white mist was.

"Hit it!" Simon yelled, and cast around for something he could throw through the portal. Cat whacked the creature hard on the nose with the toilet brush. It withdrew – and at the same moment Simon hurled one of his slippers through the portal. The misty doorway disappeared with a *pop!* and they were left looking at each other with a mixture of relief and horror.

Cat sat down on the floor, hugging the towel to herself.

"What *was* that?" she said in a faint voice.

Simon made a face. "Horrible, whatever it was. I can't believe that was the kingdom! Surely someone would have mentioned there were swamp monsters and red trees…"

"But I thought you said objects open a portal to their world – wherever they came from? Maybe they *do* have swamp monsters. Maybe they're just so used to them they didn't think it was worth mentioning?"

Simon swallowed. His eagerness to see the place where his dad had grown up was starting to diminish. No wonder Dad and Uncle Lou had decided to stay in this world, once they found it, he thought. Central heating, computer games and no evil red-eyed serpents with a mouthful of knives for teeth.

"Shall we – er – do you want to try again?" he said, looking at Cat doubtfully.

She considered. "I'm beginning to wonder whether I should try to get the hang of the spell myself – maybe you're doing it wrong. I mean, you're obviously making a portal. But I don't think Frizzle came from that swamp place – he's too furry, and he was dry when he arrived. So that means you've opened a door to two separate places so far, and neither of them looked much like the kingdom…"

"They must be the kingdom," said Simon defensively. "That's how it works! But just – I don't know – different bits? Maybe we should try one more time?"

Cat rubbed her nose thoughtfully. "OK. But we need some way to shut it quickly if it's at all dangerous."

Simon waved his other slipper. "Throwing the slipper through seemed to do it last time. It obviously closes automatically after it's been used. And I've lost one – may as well use the other one now. They're getting a bit small, anyway."

Cat looked at his rather ragged tartan slipper and giggled. "I wonder what the swamp monster is making of it."

"Hope he chokes," said Simon.

"Right," said Cat. "One more go – but then we have to think of something else. Mum is going to get a bit suspicious if too many things go missing."

Simon picked up the sword again, rather gingerly, and started to feel for the portal magic. Maybe if he really focused on the kingdom, he thought. If he imagined the castle, swords, knights and… *normal* trees. Gradually the white mist started to appear, and the wisps became firmer. Cat stood ready, and when the doorway seemed to be complete she handed the slipper to Simon, took a firm grasp of the bath towel and stuck her head into the mist.

"Hey! This is much better," she called. "It's sunny – and green – and… well… it's not exactly a *castle* but…"

She brought her head back in. "I think it's safe. Have a look."

Simon took hold of her arm to steady himself and then pushed his top half through the mist. Cat was right – it was sunny. It was pretty warm, in fact, and the sky was a fierce blue. A level green lawn stretched in front of Simon and at the end of it a huge building rose up, sheer and flat and shining in the sun. It appeared to be made of some kind of dark reflective glass, with strange metal struts extending outwards at intervals. Beyond it Simon could see other buildings made of similar shining glass or metal and bright lights winking on and off. He heard a faint buzzing sound and looked up to see small metallic eggs whizzing past and weaving between the buildings. He pulled his head back.

"That is *definitely* not the kingdom," he said with conviction. "It looks like Star Fleet Academy or something. It's *way* too futuristic to be the kingdom."

Cat shook her head. "There's something really wrong with your magic, Simon. It's not getting us anywhere near the right place. We need to rethink."

"So, shall I close the portal?" said Simon, slipper at the ready. "Or shall we explore anyway?"

"Close the portal," said Cat firmly, looking at Simon's expression. "We have no idea what that world's like. Anything could happen."

Simon sighed, and threw his slipper at the white mist. But just as the mist popped out of existence, a small blue creature flew through it and into the bedroom.

Quick as a flash Cat threw the towel over it and then forced it to the ground, holding the edges of the towel firmly as the creature underneath it wriggled and flapped its wings.

"Simon!" she yelled, as one edge of the towel was pulled out of her grip and a round blue head with two tentacles attached forced its way out. Simon reached down to grab the loose bit of towel, but as he did so, the creature extracted what looked like a blue arm and waved it at him imperiously. Simon found himself unable to move.

"Fools!" said the blue creature, as he wriggled out from under the towel and shook his wings crossly. "Opening rifts to here, there and everywhere! What in the name of the Great Forest did you think you were *doing*? You might have caused a major disaster!"

Chapter Five

The imperious blue creature was about the size of a small dog, but with his wings folded away what he most resembled was a large blue caterpillar. He was, he explained, a forest agent called Caractacus.

"One of their oldest agents," he continued, releasing Simon from the immobility spell he'd put him under with a wave of one leg. "Retired – *supposed* to be, at least. But you'd think they hadn't noticed. 'Oh, Caractacus, if you could just pop over to sort out this little problem in the Aragon?'... 'Ah Caractacus, could we just ask you to run a little errand to Chandos?'... It never stops!"

He looked round at Cat and Simon crossly. He had a round, wrinkled blue face with a rather long nose and slightly bulging eyes. Two tentacles, protruding from the top of his bald head, were waving at them impatiently.

"Now," he said, giving them both a hard stare. "I think we need to have a little talk. All this opening of ways to other worlds is not on."

"But – how did you know we were…?" said Simon. "And how did you get here so quickly?"

Caractacus snorted. "Opening a way between two worlds rips a hole in the boundary of both of them. And you've opened three in quick succession! Did you think that was the sort of thing the forest folk wouldn't *notice*? The Great Tree feels every shiver in the fabric of the worlds. That's why we have agents – so we can direct them to deal with any untoward rips or tears. It just so happens that your particular agent is currently absent."

"You mean Albert Jemmet," said Cat. "He went to the kingdom, last week."

"He did indeed," said Caractacus. "And just now he's on another errand. So they sent me." He bowed.

Cat returned a rather apologetic sort of half bow. She wasn't quite sure what to do next, so she said, tentatively, "Um, can I get you something to eat or drink?"

Caractacus nodded and looked a little more friendly. "A few leaves and some water would be most appreciated. And then we *really* need to have that little talk."

Cat hurried down to the kitchen. She scavenged in the fridge for some leftover salad and got herself and Simon a drink. Just as she left she grabbed a packet of biscuits. She had a feeling they might need some sustenance to get them through Caractacus's 'little talk'.

She was right. Caractacus insisted on taking them right back to the beginning – of all the worlds.

"The Great Tree grew out of the endless ice and darkness," he said, as if reciting from a story. "And around it grew the forest, and in its branches grew all the many worlds of light. And many and marvellous those worlds were – worlds of deserts, worlds of snow-topped mountains and deep valleys, worlds of little islands –"

"And our world is just one of them?" said Simon.

"– worlds of little islands scattered over bright

seas," went on Caractacus, ignoring him. "But the creatures of the dark resented the way their realm was being constantly pushed back by the growth of the worlds of light. They wanted to destroy the Tree. So the tree guardians and those creatures and humans who had some magic –"

"They became the forest agents!" said Simon. "Didn't they?"

Caractacus paused long enough to fix Simon with a baleful glare, and then went on intoning: "– joined together to protect the Tree and fight the ice and darkness. Until one day, there arose an enemy so powerful that the forest agents were nearly overwhelmed and the Tree destroyed…" He broke off, and in a more normal voice, added, "I was just a young whippersnapper in those days, a mere fledgling magic-user, but I remember it as if it were yesterday… the fear that fell over the forest when the name of Lukos, Lord of Wolves, was whispered." He held up one leg and waggled it at them both. "You have no idea how hard we fought, and how close it was. Why, I remember –"

"We know about this!" interrupted Simon eagerly. "Albert told us. And we know about how the king, Bruni, made the amber crown to defeat

Lukos, and that's where the deep amber comes from. If someone could gather all the amber, they could remake the crown and use it to rule all the worlds. That's why it's so important to find the other bits of amber before Lord Ravenglass does..."

He trailed off, fixed with an awful stare by Caractacus. Cat wanted to giggle but didn't dare in case the stare was turned on her next.

"You know all this," said Caractacus deliberately, with a wave of his tentacles. "Of course you do. That's why you are so eager to attract all the forces of darkness to your bedroom, no doubt. *Using* the amber! Opening ways to so many different worlds! What were you *thinking*?"

Simon frowned. "But we didn't use the amber. We were using the sword. We were trying to get to the kingdom."

Caractacus looked completely taken aback.

"The sword?" he said. He turned to Cat. "You weren't using the amber?"

"No," she said. She felt for the chain around her neck, and pulled the beautiful yellow-orange jewel out from under her T-shirt. "I wasn't even touching it – and I didn't feel it get hot or anything. Simon was the one doing the magic." She looked over at him. "I told you that you were doing it wrong," she said accusingly. "They *were* different worlds!"

Simon shrugged. "I was doing what Dora showed me. It seemed to work. I thought objects made portals to where they came from?"

"They do – usually," said Caractacus, with a frown. "This sword – it's the one that belonged to your father, I take it? Gwyn Arnold's sword. Perhaps I should have a look at it."

Simon passed it over and Caractacus felt along its length with each of his legs in turn, and then squinted at the carvings on the blade. After a while he looked up. His expression was hard to read.

"Interesting," he said.

There was a long pause while Cat and Simon looked at each other and then at Caractacus. He seemed lost in thought.

"Um – interesting how?" said Cat eventually.

Caractacus looked startled at the sound of her voice, and then waved one of his legs distractedly.

"It's a very ancient sword. And there's only one sword I know of that could open a portal to more than one world…" He trailed off, and then fixed them both with his piercing golden eyes. After a moment he seemed to come to a decision.

"We need to take it to the forest. It will have to be examined."

Simon reached out for the sword, and put a protective hand on its hilt.

"It's mine," he said. "If you're taking it to the forest, you'll have to take me, too."

Caractacus uncurled his long, caterpillar-like body, and wriggled his tentacles at Simon.

"Of course, foolish boy," he said. "You've proved yourself no end of trouble, opening portals to all those worlds. Best off in the forest where we can keep an eye on you!"

"If Simon's going, you'll have to take me, too," said Cat swiftly. There was no way she was letting Simon go off on his own. For one thing, it wasn't safe, and for another, she wasn't going to be left out of any adventure that might be had.

Caractacus turned to her with a bow. "Naturally you must come too," he said. "The wielder of the earth amber. I think on the whole it's best you are both in the forest. Things seem to be moving very quickly now. Ravenglass and his henchmen are everywhere, and we can't afford any mishaps. Too much is at stake."

As he spoke, the light in the room appeared to dim, and Cat felt a slight shiver come over her. It had seemed a bit of a game, trying to use magic and find a way to the kingdom. But Caractacus's words had reminded her of just what was out there, the powers that were ranged against them – the danger to their world, and all the others, from Lord Ravenglass and the dark crow men.

"When – when should we go?" she said. "And what are we going to tell Mum?"

"Ah, yes, your mother," said Caractacus thoughtfully. "I think maybe a little enchantment may be necessary."

It was early evening by the time Florence Arnold came home from the museum. Cat and Simon had packed small rucksacks to take with them, and Simon had put Frizzle safely in his cage and left him with some extra food.

"Frizzle?" Caractacus said with a snort. "You kept a flying margravet from Tallatertius and you called him *Frizzle*?"

"He likes it," Simon said defensively, tickling Frizzle under the chin.

Caractacus sighed and waved one leg at them both. "Well, I daresay he does. Tallatertius is a rather unpleasant world, all things considered. Being called Frizzle and having to live in a cage is probably a small price to pay for not being eaten by a glauraptor."

All that remained was to say goodbye to Florence and make sure she wouldn't worry about their absence. Cat felt rather nervous as her mum walked into the kitchen and dumped her work bag on the table with a sigh.

"Er – cup of tea, Mum?" she said, and Florence looked over gratefully.

"That would be nice," she said, and then she saw Caractacus and frowned. "What the –?"

Caractacus waved an imperious tentacle at her and muttered a few strange-sounding words.

"There's no need to be concerned," he instructed her in a firm voice. "Catrin and Simon are going on a school trip. It's all been arranged."

For a moment Cat thought it wasn't going to work. There was something rather odd about Mum's expression as she looked at the blue caterpillar. But as he spoke, her face gradually cleared, and she smiled.

"Of course," she said. "I'd forgotten. Have you got your bags packed, darlings?"

Cat nodded. She hated having to deceive Mum like this – it felt quite wrong. But on the other hand, they were finally going to the kingdom. They'd be travelling to the land where their dad had grown up, finding out more about who he had really been. Cat reached for the amber round her neck. It felt comforting in her hand. She knew it had immense power, and she knew that if need be, she could use it to protect them, herself and Simon – and whoever else needed it. She smiled at Mum and gave her a big hug.

"Bye," she said. "I love you."

Florence smiled down at her. "I love you too. Have a brilliant time. And look after Simon."

"Of course!" said Cat indignantly. "I always look after Simon."

Florence laughed and turned to Simon. "Be good," she said.

Simon gave her a big hug, and then another for luck.

"I'm *always* good!" he said with a grin.

"Well, we must be off," said Caractacus briskly and waved vaguely at the back door to the garden. "We'll be back when... well... when we're back."

"Have a lovely time!" said Florence. "See you soon!"

Simon moved eagerly to the door and Cat followed. She was excited to be going, but there was something that was bothering her, something to do with her mum's expression when she first saw Caractacus. As Cat thought about it, she suddenly realised what it was. For a moment, Mum had almost looked as if she'd *recognised* him... and the shock on her face had been tinged with fear. Cat shook her head. She must have imagined it, surely? She took a deep breath and walked through the back door, out of the kitchen and into another world entirely.

PART THREE

Chapter Six

The Druid was haggling over a richly embroidered waistcoat with a large, jovial-looking stallholder.

"But sir, observe," said the stallholder, stroking the fine material with a calloused thumb. "The close weave, the excellence of the embroidery, and," he lowered his voice, "*the extreme stupidity of your arrival here...* leaves me at a loss for words!" He raised one dark eyebrow at the Druid and surreptitiously wiped beads of sweat from his forehead with a cotton handkerchief.

"You call this fine embroidery?" said the Druid loudly, with a glance sideways at a small buzzing machine that flew past their heads and then continued weaving down the narrow lane. "Why, my mother could have done better with all her fingers tied together with catgut... And *it is indeed a foolish adventure, my friend, but I am,*" he took a quick look around and leant further over the stall, "*in a bit of a fix. Is there somewhere we can go?*"

"Twelve, you say?" said the stallholder in a tone of outrage. "I cannot accept less than thirty Sumerian shillings for this finely crafted piece. But if you wish to spend *less* money I can, ahem –" he coughed and gestured to a curtain behind the stall – "show you a few less extravagant items?"

The Druid nodded, and the man clapped his hands loudly. "Ishmel – come and mind the stall!" he called, and a thin man with a drooping face dipped his head out from behind the curtain.

"But, Rahul, I am right in the middle of a calculation," he objected.

"Mind the stall!" said Rahul firmly with a nod at the Druid. The other man's eyes widened, and he stepped out of the small booth behind the stall and took his place, calling to the passers-by, "Fine embroideries, ladies and gentlemen! Fine embroideries from the far north – you won't get better or cheaper!"

Rahul gestured for the Druid to follow him,

and then slipped into the small, dark booth and threw himself onto a pile of cushions, wiping his forehead and taking a deep breath.

"Sargon's Holy Beard! When I saw that spycopter passing I nearly died. What possessed you to come back?"

The Druid folded his long legs under him and joined Rahul on the cushions with a sigh.

"It's not by choice, believe me," he said heavily. "Only the greatest need would send me back here after last time. Tell me – is Ra-Kaleel still Chief Ensi of the city?"

Rahul mopped his forehead again and nodded, settling his bulk more comfortably on the cushions.

"He is. But even if he wasn't – twenty years is not long enough for the authorities to have forgiven you, my friend. The Akkadian Empire bears its grudges for millennia!"

He sighed, and then reached forward and clasped the Druid by the shoulders, looking at him very solemnly.

"It is good to see you, brother," he said. "Despite the danger." He enveloped the Druid in a warm embrace. The Druid found his nose squashed against the rich embroidery of Rahul's waistcoat, inhaling the spicy smells of sandalwood and cedar that he associated with this particular corner of the Grand Akkadian Empire.

At last Rahul let him go and reached for a tray on which were set several ornate glasses and a brass teapot very like the one the Druid had in his pack. He poured a rich dark-green liquid into two glasses and passed one to the Druid.

"To your health – may your shadow never grow short," he said, lifting his glass. His wide smile made the corners of his eyes crinkle up into deep folds and his snaggly brown teeth made him look suddenly villainous. "To the legendary Thieves of Ur!" he said, and drained his glass in one gulp.

The Druid raised his glass with a wry smile and drained it, slapping the glass down on the tray with a ringing sound.

"To the Thieves of Ur," he said, and then, leaning forward, his eyes starting to lose their focus, he slurred, "Do they still… thieve?"

"Why, yes, of course!" said Rahul, as the Druid slumped across the cushions in front of him, unconscious. "We thieve – as always – for the person with the highest price to offer…"

Ra-Kaleel, Chief Ensi of the Imperial City of Ur-Akkad, and thus second only in power to the Sargon, was sipping a glass of mint tea thoughtfully and trying to work out why he had a niggling sense of unease. The palace was quiet – the Ninety-ninth Sargon was on his annual pilgrimage to the Holy City of Atlantis and half the court had gone with him. This had given Ra-Kaleel, as it did every year, the opportunity to tighten discipline in the troops and reinforce strict laws of obedience among the population of the city. As a result, everyone was too terrified to put a foot out of place and the court and temples were running smoothly, just as the Chief Ensi liked it.

No, it wasn't discipline that was the problem. It was something else. Something in the air. A sense of untamed magic, somewhere outside the channels of containment Akkad had used to control magic for generations. Maybe there was a renegade magic-user at large in the city, despite all his efforts. Maybe one had arrived from outside the Empire…?

Ra-Kaleel smiled. It made his thin, stretched face look a little like a snake's. He would enjoy hunting out a new magic-user. It was a long time since he'd had the chance to use the might of the Akkadian Empire to crush an outcast enemy of the Sargon.

He clapped his hands and summoned the captain of the guards, a short, stocky man of Babylonian extraction.

"Timon, we have an enemy at large. I can feel it. Somewhere close. Bring me the chief spymaster – I want every soldier on his guard, every informer alerted, every priest in the temples on watch. I want the movements of every creature in the city recorded and checked by the spycopters for unusual activity. If there's a new rat in the palace sewer – if the bakery on New Moon Street makes two extra loaves of bread – if a spider so much as builds its web in a different corner of the meanest hovel in the Potter's Quarter, I want to know. *Do you understand?*"

The captain looked startled, but he bowed his head immediately. "It shall be as you wish, O great Ensi."

Ra-Kaleel's dark eyes glittered. "If you value your life," he said, and smiled.

Chapter Seven

The decorated tile that Dora and Jem had used to make a portal had once adorned the wall of the robing room in the Temple of Ishtar at the centre of the noble and imperial city of Ur-Akkad. So that was where the portal took them. The room was small and dimly lit, filled with long racks of embroidered robes and headdresses. Luckily for Jem and Dora, Ishtar was not the favoured goddess of the current Sargon, who preferred the warrior god, Ababaza, and had shifted most of his priests and officials to the rival temple complex on the other side of the city. Still, there was a full complement of temple servants and a number of dedicated priests and priestesses. So Jem and Dora barely had time to adjust their eyes to the gloom in the robing room before the door opened, and a rather startled voice called out in surprise.

"Who – who are you? What are you doing here?"

"We got lost," said Jem confidently. "Sorry. Any chance you could show us the way out?"

The figure standing in the doorway was a girl. She was taller than Dora – about the same height as Jem – and she was wearing a plain white dress and leather sandals. Her dark hair was braided, with bright jewels and beads threaded into it, and her skin was the soft black colour of a night sky. She gave Dora and Jem a swift once-over and then shut the door behind her and pressed her hand against the wall. Instantly the room lit up with a bright yellow light – it was as if the girl had opened a large window and let in the glare of the midday sun. Jem gasped, and Dora tried to work out if the girl had used a spell, but it didn't feel like it. It was more like the – what was it? – the *electricity* they'd seen in Simon and Cat's world. But there was a muted feel of magic about the place, Dora was sure.

There was a knock at the door and an imperious voice from beyond it.

"Inanna! Have you got the robes? Hurry up!"

"Just a minute!" the girl called back. "Nearly there..."

She put her finger to her lips, and gestured for Dora and Jem to follow her. Hurrying across the room she reached the opposite wall, which was decorated with a large relief carving of a city scene. Taking firm hold of a protruding spire from one of the buildings, she twisted, and a long upright crack appeared across the relief. She pulled at it and a door slid back, revealing a dark passage.

"In there!" hissed the girl. "Wait for me!" She pushed Dora and Jem towards it urgently, and then ran back to the other door and slipped out, grabbing a couple of long silvery robes on her way.

Dora looked at Jem and raised her eyebrows. He shrugged. "She's seen us and she hasn't raised the alarm. We may as well do what she says, for now."

Dora nodded, and the two of them slipped into the dark passageway and waited.

It wasn't long before the girl returned, closing the door to the robing room after her and dousing the light with a flick of her hand. She followed them into the passageway and then slid the fake wall shut with a click. Dora was surprised to find that the passageway was not completely dark – a faint glow from somewhere above was making it possible to see Jem's face next to her, and the white dress of their guide.

"Stay quiet!" the girl whispered to them. "Follow me..."

As they set off up the passage, Jem sidled up to Dora and hissed in her ear. "My mouth feels funny. When we talk. It doesn't feel quite right."

Dora looked at him in puzzlement. "Your *mouth* feels funny?" she started to say, and then stopped and frowned. "That's really..." She stopped again, and then put her hands up to her mouth and felt her lips. Jem was right. When she talked, it was as if her mouth was making odd shapes – her tongue moving differently, the breath being forced out of her lips in a way that didn't feel quite right. As they stared at each other in consternation, the girl noticed that they had stopped and slipped back to pull at their clothes.

"Come on!" she said. "It's not safe here! The Ensi use these passages. We need to get to my chambers."

"Ensi?" said Jem.

"The Sargon's officials. They run the place – and they don't like having strangers arrive out of nowhere!"

After a few more twists and turns, and a number of narrow stairways, the girl reached what appeared to be a dead end. She pushed hard on a single blue jewel set into the end wall of the passage and another door slid across. Beyond it was a beautifully furnished, light, airy room, with silk hangings on the wall, dark carved wooden chairs with embroidered cushion seats, and a huge arched window open to the blue sky.

"My room," said the girl, and gestured at the window. "Take a look. But be careful – watch out for the spycopters."

"Spycopters?" said Jem, as he headed for the window. "What are they?"

The girl frowned. "Don't you know *anything*?" she said. "The Ensi's spying machines – they fly around the city, watching everything, and recording it. If you see one, duck back inside."

Dora moved hesitantly to the window. She didn't like the sound of the spycopters, but she was curious to see the city they'd arrived in. As she cautiously leant out, she couldn't help gaping. They were at the top of a high tower, and stretching out below them was a vast city. There were thousands of buildings of red sandstone and white marble all jumbled together, with dazzling spires and towers right across the city, all reaching up into the deep blue sky. In amongst the buildings she could see the tops of trees, their dark green leaves shading the streets below, and hear the faint bustle of crowds, the calls of stallholders, bells ringing, and the faraway sound of music. In some ways it reminded her of the bustle and grand jumble of buildings in the kingdom's capital city. But the shapes of the houses were different, and she could see tiny closed carts down on the street that appeared to be moving without any horses pulling them. The smell was different, too – a rich, unfamiliar smell, a little like lemons, with a hint of cloves and vanilla. It was quite unlike the predominant smell of pigs she associated with the kingdom.

She glanced sideways at Jem, who was drinking in the sights of the new world with an eager expression, and he grinned at her. Whatever her own doubts and worries about what they had done, Jem was in his element.

She turned back to the girl with the braids and bobbed a curtsey.

"My name is Dora," she said, trying to ignore the slightly odd feeling in her mouth as she spoke. "This is Jem. We're not exactly sure where we are – we're looking for a friend."

The girl stood very straight and poised, her dark brown eyes regarding them solemnly. "You are in the most high Temple of Ishtar, in the city of Ur-Akkad, first city of the glorious Akkadian Empire. I am Princess Inanna, priestess-daughter of the Ninety-ninth Sargon, ruler of Akkad and High Lord of the Universe." She nodded at them, and then grinned. "And you are clearly from another world. My summoning spell brought you – I felt it working! You're a little younger than I was hoping for – but no matter. You will take me away from this world, before they find I'm a magic-user and imprison me!"

Chapter Eight

Something was not right.

The Druid felt as if his head was inside a dragon's mouth. Its hot breath was making him feel distinctly uncomfortable and its rasping tongue was pulling at his skin painfully. In addition, it kept shifting its weight and at least part of it appeared to be sitting on him. He tried to lift his arms, but they seemed to have disappeared. Instead, two white fish were weaving around in front of his eyes and every now and again one of them came close and slapped him on the cheek with its tail. It was all rather peculiar.

The Druid tried to close his eyes and then realised that they *were* closed. So he tried to open them. It felt as if someone had pressed a handful of wet clay over his eyelids and now it had dried solid.

The dragon appeared to have finally given up licking him, but now he could hear the faint sound of voices echoing around his head.

"He's awake – moving."

"Slap him again."

The Druid felt a sharp slap on his face. He drew in his breath and made a huge effort to open his eyes.

He was lying on the floor of a cave with a roaring fire close by, and Rahul and Ishmel were peering down at him anxiously.

"Aha!" said Rahul, and clapped his hands. "You are awake!"

"You *drugged* me!" said the Druid, outraged.

"A thousand apologies, my friend!" said Rahul, making a comically mournful face. "But to transport you here it was necessary that you were unconscious. No one may see the route to the Thieves' Cave... Even a very old friend and ally of the Thieves, such as yourself!"

The Druid started to lift himself off the floor, patting his face tentatively.

"Worlds above! What did you give me? It feels as if I've been pummelled by a troll. Couldn't you just have told me not to look?"

Rahul shrugged apologetically. "I couldn't even tell you I was giving you the potion, my friend. You could have cast a spell so it didn't work. The lord commander is very strict about the rules."

"Here," said Ishmel, passing the Druid a glass filled with a hot, dark liquid. "This will make you feel better."

The Druid looked at it dubiously.

Ishmel grinned. "Really – it will help."

The Druid downed the glass in one and then nodded. "Excellent! Spiced Sumerian wine. *Almost* enough to make up for your utter treachery. Now, tell me – who is the current lord commander, and can I see him? It's most urgent."

Across the city, in the Temple of Ishtar, Dora and Jem were tucking into a feast. Princess Inanna's chambers were equipped with everything she would need for a full week's holy retreat – something the priestesses of Ishtar were expected to do whenever they got the call from the goddess. As Dora remarked, this meant she had just about enough food to keep Jem going for a day.

"At least we're safe here – and we have a bit of time to make plans," said Jem, his mouth full of a rather delicious savoury pastry Inanna had offered them.

As he swallowed, Inanna handed him a soft yellow fruit and a flat piece of some kind of bread. She seemed fascinated by just how much food Jem was capable of putting away and had been pressing new delicacies on him constantly since they'd started eating.

"Jem – you'll explode if you eat any more," said Dora, rolling her eyes, and he gave her a sheepish grin and waved the fruit and bread aside. Inanna put it back down on the tray between them, looking faintly disappointed.

"So, what exactly are we planning?" asked Dora.

"You are here to help me," said Inanna firmly. "That's what I summoned you for!"

"First of all, you didn't summon us – we came ourselves," said Dora, equally firmly. "And secondly, we have to find the Druid, and… something else we came for. Don't we, Jem?" She nudged Jem with her foot.

"Yes, we do," he said obediently, and then stopped. He put his hand up to his mouth and repeated, "Yes… we… do…"

He turned to her with a grin.

"Dora!" he said in excitement. "I've worked it out! Our mouths feel funny because we're talking in a different language! It must be something to do with the portal magic. It makes you speak the language of wherever you end up!"

Inanna frowned. "You are speaking the language of Ur-Akkad, of course. Surely you knew that?"

"No," said Jem. "To us it feels just like we're speaking the language of the kingdom – but if you really concentrate, you can tell the words are different."

Dora thought about it.

"Jem," she said, experimentally. It sounded the same as usual – but then it would, she realised, because it was his name. "Jem is a fat pig with no manners," she said, and then laughed. He was right! If she concentrated on what was coming out of her mouth, the words were completely strange. But their meaning seemed as clear to her as the words of the kingdom.

"How did we never notice this in Simon and Cat's world?" she said.

Jem shrugged. "Maybe we were too busy

running after Sir Bedwyr, or fighting Smith and Jones. Or maybe their language is closer to ours, so it didn't feel so odd."

Inanna clapped her hands imperiously.

"Enough! We must proceed. We must work out how I can get away from here! Jem…" She took his hand and squeezed it hard. "You *will* help me, won't you? In a fortnight's time I'll be fourteen and I'll have to leave the Temple. I'll have to go to the household of Ra-Kaleel, the Chief Ensi. The second princess always runs the Chief Ensi's household. But I can't do it! It's too dangerous! He'll realise I'm a magic-user!" Her voice had more than a hint of a sob in it, and her eyes were liquid and pleading as they gazed intently into Jem's.

Dora snorted. She could see Jem blushing and she knew that Inanna had chosen exactly the right strategy to get what she wanted. Jem's dearest ambition had always been to be a knight and rescue beautiful damsels.

"O-of course," stammered Jem, squeezing Inanna's hand in return. "We'll… we'll do our best. But why does it matter if he finds out you can use magic?"

"Magic is not allowed in the Akkadian Empire," said Inanna. "At least, not free magic." For the first time real fear seemed to enter her eyes.

"What do you mean?" said Dora.

"Magic-users are imprisoned," said Inanna, with a wobble in her voice. "Their magic is extracted by a machine the Ensi have built – it's used to power the city. The magic is piped into houses for the lights and fans, and it's used to power the spycopters, to keep the horseless chariots running, and for weapons. The magic-users, they... they never see daylight again."

"But that's terrible!" said Dora, shocked. "*Anyone?* Any magic-user? How do they find them?"

Inanna shuddered. "The Ensi have ways – there are spies, informers. No one dares to even talk about it. My mother, when she realised I had magic... she gave me secret books, she taught me some spells, but she also taught me to never, ever let my magic show, never use it except in emergencies. But she died, and I was sent to the Temple. And now I'm nearly fourteen and I have to go to Ra-Kaleel's household. I *can't* go there – I *can't*! So I made a summoning spell to bring someone from another world, so they could take me back with them. Anywhere – so long as it's away from here."

Her last words were half whispered. Jem gave her an awkward pat on the back. "Don't worry. Of course we'll take you back with us," he said reassuringly. "Won't we, Dora?"

Dora bit her lip and nodded. "But we need to find the Druid – and we need to do it soon, before this Ra-Kaleel finds out we're here and hooks us up to his horrible machine." She shivered, thinking about the many people that must be imprisoned in the city, helpless, their magic siphoned off into secret channels to power the strange lighting and the spycopters.

"If we want to find the Druid," said Jem thoughtfully, with a glance at Inanna, "then we probably need to start by looking for the amber."

"Jem!" said Dora, horrified. "You shouldn't –"

"We're going to have to trust her," said Jem. "We'll find the Druid and the amber much quicker with Inanna's help. And the sooner we find the amber, the sooner she gets to escape."

"Find the amber?" said Inanna, with a frown.

"Have you heard anything about it?" said Jem eagerly. "A powerful jewel – a piece of deep amber. There's a piece in this world somewhere. It's what we came to get."

Inanna hesitated. "There is a jewel – I've heard it spoken of. There's an old saying that the dragon's amber is the heart of the empire. But I thought it was just a legend…"

"That could be it," said Jem. "But do any of the stories say where it might be?"

Inanna hesitated. "There's a book my mother gave me. It's very old. It has a poem about the dragon's amber – but I don't think it makes much sense…"

She reached under her bed and pulled out a plain wooden chest. Unlocking it with a small key she kept round her neck, she drew out an old book with torn and stained pages. Jem and Dora moved forward eagerly and craned over her shoulders as she flicked through the book until she reached a poem near the centre. It was written in deep black ink, and decorated around the edges with richly coloured and fantastical drawings of dragons.

Only obsidian
Cuts through the skin
Of the dragon's fire amber,
Hidden within.

Down through the Lapis Gate,
Down in the deep
Dragon's dark labyrinth,
There let them weep.

There was a moment's silence.

"What in the forest's name is that supposed to mean?" said Jem, exasperated.

"Do you have any idea?" Dora asked Inanna.

She frowned, thinking. "The Lapis Gate is the east gate of the city – it's decorated with lapis lazuli. It's quite close to the temple. I suppose it's possible there's an entrance there to some kind of labyrinth... It's part of the Old City, and there are any number of secret tunnels and passageways between the buildings."

"Where there are dragons?" said Jem, starting to look excited.

"I've never heard that there are dragons under the city," said Inanna doubtfully. "But we do have dragons out in the desert. In the old days they were sometimes used to guard very precious treasures."

"And obsidian does cut dragon's skin," said Dora. "It's the only thing that does. But what does it mean, *There let them weep*?"

They looked at each other, wondering about what might be waiting for them, even if they could find their way to this labyrinth. Dora hoped fervently that the mention of dragons was just a myth to scare away anyone who might try to steal the amber.

Inanna stood up. "Come on," she said. "If we're going to find this labyrinth then we'd better have obsidian knives. And I know just where to find them!"

Jem and Dora had never seen so much gold in their lives as there was in the treasury of the Temple of Ishtar. Inanna had brought them there by another of the twisting dark passages that riddled the temple, and now she was searching quickly and quietly through the wooden chests in the corner.

"How do you know your way through all these

passages?" Jem asked, as they followed her into the dimly lit chamber.

"I have lived in the temple since I was eight," Inanna replied, feeling for the right knob to open the chest in front of her. "I was shown one passage – as a quick route between my chamber and the shrine – but I was commanded not to enter any of the other passages. So I made sure I explored them every time I had a spare afternoon. I've never really liked doing what I'm told." She grinned at them both, her teeth like faint pearls shining in the dark shadows.

She's just like Jem, thought Dora. He never does what he's told either.

A few moments later, Inanna had found what she was looking for, and she headed back to them in triumph with three extremely wicked-looking dark obsidian blades. Handing two of them to Jem and Dora, she tucked one carefully into the belt of her dress.

"Now – I'll take you to the robing room," whispered Inanna. "To get you dressed in something a little less foreign."

This was a sound idea, but it fell foul of Jem's fascination with armour. The minute he spotted the silvery breastplate and helmet hanging in the corner of the robing room, he was determined to wear it.

"But it's the uniform of an imperial guard!" said Inanna.

"So?" said Jem. "Even better – no one will question us!"

"If we meet any officers they might ask your name, or rank, or send you to some other guard post. It's not exactly inconspicuous!" said Dora, exasperated.

Jem turned to Inanna. "Who's the most important person in the palace?" he said.

"The Sargon, of course," said Inanna instantly. "But when he's away, it's Ra-Kaleel."

"Then I'll just say I'm on a secret mission for the Great Ensi, Ra-Kaleel, and no one is to hinder me if they value their life," said Jem loftily.

Inanna put her head on one side and contemplated him with a frown.

"It *might* work," she said. "Try strutting a little – as if you're really important."

Jem added a little swagger to his gait and saluted them both, and Inanna clapped her hands.

"Perfect!" she said. "And the uniform *does* suit you!"

Dora snorted, and picked the darkest, plainest robe she could from the hooks on the wall.

"Come on, then," she said. "We need to head for the Lapis Gate. If we use the secret passages and stay out of sight as much as possible, we may not get stopped."

But as they left, Dora was aware of something niggling at the back of her mind. Something to do with Inanna's summoning spell. The spell hadn't been responsible for bringing her and Jem to this world because they'd been coming already. But Inanna had said she'd felt it work. So it must have summoned *someone*. The question was, who?

Chapter Nine

Mr Smith and Mr Jones were stalking through the dark streets of Novoridad when they felt the tug of a powerful summoning spell.

"Ow!" said Mr Smith, the shinier and smoother of the two tall, thin men in black suits.

Mr Jones, the older and dustier of the two, stopped, and sniffed the air.

"It came from the Akkadian Empire," he said in a rasping voice. His black eyes glittered. "We haven't tried *there* yet, Mr Smith."

Mr Smith stretched his thin lips into a cold smile. "Indeed we have not, Mr Jones, indeed we have not. Maybe something's afoot. What do you say?"

Mr Jones considered. "We'll accept the summoning, then," he said with a short nod.

The two dark figures strode out into the city square, leaving the narrow alley where they had been empty and silent.

Ra-Kaleel returned to the palace from an inspection of the city guard, hoping for a quiet hour and a reviving goblet of Byzantine mead. He was disconcerted to find Mr Smith and Mr Jones in his audience chamber.

"What in the Sargon's name are *you* doing here?" he said, looking at the tall black-suited men with distaste. "We paid you well for your work and told you never to return."

"You sent for us," rasped Mr Jones, frowning. "A summoning. We came as soon as we could."

The Chief Ensi frowned back. "I most certainly did not send for you," he said. "I have no need of your services any more. I am capable of dealing with any renegade magic-users on my own."

Mr Smith glanced at his companion and held his hand up soothingly. "We are aware of your much increased mightiness, O great Ensi," he said with a slight bow. "But there was a spell, and it came from your empire."

"Well, it was not from me," said Ra-Kaleel petulantly.

Mr Jones put his head on one side and looked hard at the Ensi with one bright black eye.

"It was, now I think of it, a slightly... uncoordinated summoning. A general call. It may have caught us by accident rather than design."

He turned to Mr Smith. "There's something here, I can feel it. There's kingdom magic somewhere near, or my name's not Jones."

Mr Smith grinned nastily. "Which it most certainly is, eh, Mr Jones?" He laughed a rattling laugh and turned to Ra-Kaleel. "Someone summoned us. And now we're here, I have a feeling we may be in exactly the right place... We're after a piece of *deep amber*."

He watched Ra-Kaleel attentively as he spoke, but the Ensi was utterly impassive. *Too impassive*, thought Mr Smith.

Ra-Kaleel barely raised an eyebrow as he replied. "You're mistaken if you think we have anything of that sort in the Akkadian Empire. I'm afraid your trip has been wasted, my friends."

Mr Smith glanced at Mr Jones, and he nodded. The two of them moved towards the Chief Ensi so fast that he had no chance to react. At the same time, a wave of Mr Jones's hand caused the door of the great audience chamber to slam shut. The guards standing at various points around the room all slumped to the ground, completely unconscious.

"*We are not your friends*," said Mr Smith gently, his lips almost touching the Chief Ensi's ear. "We are here for the deep amber and you – who so obviously know exactly what we're talking about – *you* are going to show us where to find it."

"But first," whispered Mr Jones lovingly into Ra-Kaleel's other ear, "you are going to explain why we can taste kingdom magic in this world where there shouldn't be any."

Ra-Kaleel held himself still, trying not to show the fear drenching his body. Mr Smith and Mr Jones had been very useful hired hands some years ago, when there had been a small rebellion of magic-users, but he'd been glad when their contract had ended and they'd disappeared back to whatever dark world they came from. Now they'd returned, and they wanted the deep amber... Ra-Kaleel knew he should defend the dragon stone with his life rather than let it fall into an outsider's hands. But his legs felt like water and the hot breath of the two men in each ear felt like the burning fires of the afterlife. Ra-Kaleel closed his eyes and resigned himself to his treachery.

"The magic you have detected – I noticed it yesterday. My spies have tracked the source to the caves of the Thieves of Ur. An informer has agreed to deliver the magic-user to us. As for the amber… It's here, in the palace. I can guide you to it."

"Excellent," said Mr Smith, standing up straight and patting Ra-Kaleel on the back. "Then I suggest you take us to it right now, and we'll deal with your magic-user at the same time."

He grinned at Mr Jones, and Mr Jones gave a rasping laugh. Ra-Kaleel smiled feebly, and wondered if he was going to be sick.

Not far from the palace, the guards at the Lapis Gate were looking at Jem with an air of puzzlement. The great arch in the city wall was always busy with travellers and merchants entering and leaving the city, but it was highly unusual for officers of the imperial guard to turn up and demand to be let into the locked chamber at the side of the gate.

"An errand for the Chief Ensi, you say, sir?" the taller of the two guards repeated. "We didn't hear about it. What cohort did you say you hailed from?"

Jem frowned. "It's none of your business, O most lowly of gate guards," he said, standing up straighter. "It is enough for you to know that my mission is important. If you hinder me, Ra-Kaleel shall hear of it." He leant forward and added, in a low tone, "And he won't be happy."

The gate guards hesitated. Behind Jem, Inanna had the hood of her cloak pulled well up, but Dora could see that she was looking worried. They had agreed that Jem would have to do the talking as Inanna was not supposed to leave the Temple precincts. If she was spotted in the streets, word would get back to Ra-Kaleel almost instantly. But Jem's attempt to pass himself off as one of the imperial guard was not going well.

"Hey, Jeremiah?" called the guard, as his eye swept Jem up and down. "Might need to send a message through to headquarters on this one."

A thin man, who had been recording the

goods and travellers passing through the gate into the city, looked up from his scroll and raised an eyebrow. "Trouble, Bashar?"

The tall guard looked back and forth from Jem to the scribe. "I'm not sure. This whippersnapper here wants entrance to the gate. He's claiming to be working for Ra-Kaleel, but I've not seen his face before…"

The scribe frowned and started to move towards them. Inanna whispered in Jem's ear, and he stood up straighter and accosted the guard again.

"You're wasting time!" he said in a commanding voice. "Let us through immediately. I have an urgent mission, I tell you!"

Dora could feel sweat trickling down between her shoulder blades, and it wasn't just the searing heat in the city streets that was causing it. A crowd was starting to gather as they argued with the guards, and the thin scribe, after looking suspiciously at Jem's armour, was reaching for a strange device on his desk, like a flat box lit up with green buttons.

Dora was just wondering whether to risk a spell when Inanna stepped forward. She pushed her hood back, revealing her beautiful dark hair and the shining jewels and beads braided into it.

"Enough!" she said dramatically. "It is I, Inanna, the daughter of the Sargon, ruler of the Great Empire, High Lord of the Universe. How dare you question and impede myself and my protectors? We are under direct orders from the Chief Ensi, and if you hold us here a second longer he will have you hauled to the *dungeons!*" She snapped her fingers to emphasise her point, and the gate guard blanched and bowed.

"Your Highness – of course… Please enter!"

Inanna stalked grandly past, gesturing to Jem and Dora to follow her. She halted pointedly at an ornate door in the side of the gate arch. It was small but richly decorated, covered with lapis lazuli flowers and stars.

"Open it!" she ordered, and the scribe hurried to her side with a bunch of keys. Choosing a large golden one, he unlocked the door and gestured at the small chamber within, hollowed out of one of the great columns that supported the gate.

"Your Highness," he said respectfully, and Inanna nodded to him and swept into the chamber with Jem and Dora behind her.

Once inside, they shut the door firmly and bolted it across, and only then did Dora draw breath.

"Blood and bone!" said Jem. "That was close. But we're in."

Inanna shrugged. "No thanks to you," she said with a pout. "And now they know I'm with you and not in the temple. It won't take long for Ra-Kaleel to hear of that. We'll need to hurry."

That, thought Dora, was an understatement. She was beginning to feel a sense of growing urgency. They still needed to find the Druid, and the amber, and then they had to escape from this unpleasant world with its caged, contained magic – and the quicker the better.

"So – do we know how to get into this labyrinth, now we're at the Lapis Gate?" she said, glancing anxiously back at the bolted door.

The chamber was a small square room with slit windows on the side of the gate that faced outwards from the city. It was clearly meant for defence but was also used as a general storeroom, with bits of spare armour, weapons, sacks of confiscated goods and spare scrolls scattered haphazardly around on benches and tables. Inanna tried a few knobs on the relief carvings on the walls but without success. Dora lifted a few boxes and looked behind an embroidered hanging, but she couldn't see anything that looked like a door.

"There!" said Jem at last, pointing to an old carpet on the floor. One corner had been pulled up by someone dragging a heavy chest across the floor – and just visible underneath was the edge of a trapdoor.

Together they pulled the carpet back and lifted the trapdoor. Disappearing down into the darkness was a set of worn stone steps.

"*The dragon's dark labyrinth*," breathed Inanna. "So it does exist."

"What did the poem say?" asked Dora, with a slight shake in her voice.

"*The dragon's fire amber*," said Jem. "*Hidden within…* It's down there somewhere."

"And so are the dragons," said Inanna, her eyes widening.

Dora took a deep breath and conjured a werelight, and the three of them stepped into the hole. Jem, who was at the back, let the trapdoor fall back down behind him, sealing them into the darkness.

PART FOUR

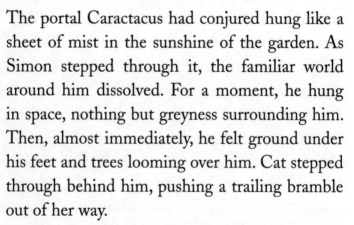

Chapter Ten

The portal Caractacus had conjured hung like a sheet of mist in the sunshine of the garden. As Simon stepped through it, the familiar world around him dissolved. For a moment, he hung in space, nothing but greyness surrounding him. Then, almost immediately, he felt ground under his feet and trees looming over him. Cat stepped through behind him, pushing a trailing bramble out of her way.

Simon could feel the magic as soon as he was through the portal. The tingle of it was all around, like a kind of music. He breathed in deeply, thinking about his dad, who'd grown up here amongst all this magic. He wondered if Dad had ever walked through this part of the Great Forest. Apart from the tingle of magic in the air,

112

it all seemed quite normal. The trees seemed to be just trees, the sky and earth and undergrowth no different from home. He glanced back at Cat and grinned.

Caractacus beckoned to them, and they started to walk deeper into the forest, following a dark, narrow path that twisted and turned endlessly. As they got further in, they began to hear strange noises, catch glimpses of things that shouldn't – couldn't – be there. Caractacus was flying ahead of them, looking less like a caterpillar and more like a small bright blue bird, leading them on into the greenish gloom.

Simon pushed aside a creeper and stopped, startled. He could have sworn that behind it was a battered green wheelie bin – but when he blinked it disappeared. Only a few steps further on they caught the sound of a station announcement through the trees: *The 14.27 from Chichester is approaching Platform Six*. And then suddenly there was a whole row of people, standing on the path in front of him.

"S-sorry!" said Simon, stopping and backing away slightly. But the people didn't respond. They appeared to be looking sideways, as if they could see something approaching, and Simon could hear the squeal of a train's brakes.

"Just ignore them," called Caractacus, flitting back to them above the people's heads. "It's another world. We can see in, but they can't see us."

As he spoke, the people faded, and there was just the rustle of branches and the sound of soft leaves underfoot.

"Sorry about that," said Caractacus. "There are always a few shifts in the forest, but it's getting worse lately. Smith and Jones have been tearing through the worlds trying to locate the missing bits of amber – leaving chaos behind them. And we haven't enough agents to see to it all, most of them are too busy searching for the amber themselves."

"Have they found any yet?" said Cat, brushing a few stray twigs out of her blonde hair as she glanced up at him.

Caractacus looked back at her with an odd expression, as if trying to decide how much to tell her. Then he nodded. "We have found one. The fire amber."

He flitted further on, and then, as they followed, he continued. "Each of the pieces of amber has an affinity for a different element –

yours is the earth amber of the north. It's the most stable and the strongest of the four. The queen has the sky amber, and for the moment she's enough in control of it that Ravenglass hasn't been able to take it from her. That might change – we'll need to think about getting her away if he gets his hands on another piece. It'll make his magic that much stronger."

"But the fire amber?" said Cat, pushing a stray branch out of her way. "Can you get it before he does?"

"We've sent an agent there. We hope he'll be able to find it before Smith and Jones get wind of anything. But the fire amber's always been a little tricky to control." He sighed. "And it's in a rather dangerous place for magic-users, unfortunately. The Akkadian Empire."

Cat frowned. "That sounds familiar somehow... Wasn't there an Akkadian Empire on our world a long time ago?"

"Yes, indeed. The two worlds overlapped for a time in that area. Commonalities, you see – both hot, dusty places, good for dragons. There was a lot more overlap, in those days, between all the worlds."

"Is that why the kingdom seems so similar to

our bit of the world?" said Simon. "Those other places we opened portals to – they were really different. But the kingdom seems much the same, except… like our past, or like fairy tales. Knights and magic and castles."

Caractacus nodded. "The kingdom's always been close to your world. Yours was one of the first worlds to be made, and there was a lot of back and forth in the early days. You gave us knowledge of metalwork and other things. Knights and so on." He screwed up his face. "Foolish ideas. And in return we showed you magic. After all the worlds became split, memories of the kingdom remained in your folk tales. The Land of Faerie, Tir-na-nog, the Otherworld – you have many names for us."

For a moment he appeared to be lost in thought, then he shook himself and fluttered to a branch on the path ahead.

"Come along, come along – we need to get to the Great Tree and show that sword to the Guardians. The worlds are shifting, I can feel it – and we must be prepared."

The Great Tree was a golden colour, and it glowed

with such a strong light that the whole clearing in which it stood seemed to be in full sunshine. Great tangled roots arched away from the enormous gnarled trunk and twisted and turned around each other before falling back down into a blanket of golden leaves. The trunk was sculpted into the strangest shapes, as if many different trees had become fused as one, all fighting to rise up and outwards, sending huge branches soaring up to the sky. But where the sky should have been, all they could see was a white, swirling mist into which the branches disappeared. It was constantly moving and changing, like cloud formations in a hurricane. It was beautiful and awesome, and it made Simon feel rather faint.

"That's the Great Tree?" he said, slightly breathlessly.

"Indeed it is," said Caractacus proudly, as if he'd planted it himself. "The World Tree – the centre of all the worlds of light."

He bowed towards the tree, and then called out impatiently. "Well – come on then! Where are you all? I've brought the children – and a rather interesting sword."

As he spoke there was a faint rustling sound,

and then from behind the tree – or was it from within? – a number of rather odd-looking people emerged. They were tall, and their skin was green and brown, flecked with gold. *The colour of leaves*, Simon thought. And then he realised that the people looked altogether like trees – and yet like people as well. He blinked.

The people – or trees – gathered around them. They came closer without Simon ever being quite sure whether he'd seen any of them walking, and afterwards he wasn't even sure how long he'd stood there while they gathered. It was like watching a clock intently and then realising the minute hand had shifted from one number to another.

"These are the children?" said one of the tree people. He (Simon was pretty sure it was a he, somehow) was browner and sturdier than most of the others and more weather-beaten. Simon found that if he concentrated hard, he could see two hazel-brown eyes regarding him questioningly. At which point he realised that he was definitely looking at a person and couldn't think why he'd ever thought it might be a tree.

"Yes, the children," said Caractacus. "I told you. And the sword that appeared in their world. Their father's sword."

The man blinked at Simon and Cat, and extended a warm brown hand to each.

"I am Rowan," he said. "I am one of the guardians. We find it hard to assume... um... human form. So generally only one of us will do so, to speak for the others."

He nodded at the gathered tree people around him, most of whom were now looking much more like trees, as if they'd temporarily lent Rowan all their more human aspects. Holding the two children's hands, he closed his eyes, and took a deep breath.

When he opened them, he looked troubled.

"You have power," he said. "You will both have an important part in what's to come. But there is a dark shadow over you. There are dangers, and choices – and things may not go well for the Great Tree if you make the wrong choice."

Simon shivered, and looked at Cat. She tried to smile, but her eyes were anxious.

Caractacus harrumphed. "Well, yes, that's as maybe, but there's no need to frighten the poor children half to death. Prophecies are all very well but preparation is better, I've always found. Now – the sword. Perhaps you could have a look?"

Rowan turned his brown eyes on Caractacus and rustled gently, as if he were laughing.

"The forest's most trusty agent," he said. "What would we do without you, Caractacus?"

"Find some other poor benighted magic-user to traipse round half the worlds on your errands, I expect," said Caractacus, with a snort. He turned to Cat and Simon. "The guardians are bound to the forest and the Tree. They can feel what the Tree feels – when there are tears or rents in the boundaries of the worlds, when they are disturbed by the forces of the dark. But they can't leave the forest. So looking after the boundaries and the balance of the worlds is the business of the forest agents, who can travel between them." He turned back to Rowan. "The sword?" he reminded him.

"Ah, yes – indeed." Rowan held out a brown hand, and Simon, slightly reluctantly, pulled the sword out from where it was tucked into his belt and passed it over.

"It was my dad's," he said. "We used it to try to

get to the kingdom – but it kept opening portals to other worlds."

"Indeed?" said Rowan, surprised. "Other worlds?" He exchanged a look with Caractacus, and then felt the sword carefully. He nodded, and then passed it back to the surrounding guardians. As they examined it, Simon thought, they seemed again to be more like people than trees, leaning in and whispering amongst themselves. When Rowan passed it back, the sword was gleaming slightly, as if it had absorbed some of the light of the Great Tree.

"It is a mighty sword," said Rowan solemnly. "We knew already that your father was a descendant of the great king, Bruni. But it seems he was an heir from the line of his youngest son, the one who stayed to fight the forces of the dark in the north. It was Bruni who originally forged this sword."

"This is Bruni's sword?" said Simon, startled. "The actual same one? The one he cut the tree with to make the amber?"

Rowan nodded.

"I thought as much," said Caractacus, with satisfaction. "Bruni's sword was made from metal taken from every world – part of every world was forged into its being. That's why it can open a portal to anywhere!"

"It is indeed forged from a part of all worlds," said Rowan. "And it has been lost for a long time. To find it again, now – that is a stroke of good fortune indeed."

"Why?" said Cat.

"Because if Lord Ravenglass succeeds in remaking the Crown," said Rowan gently, "the only way to destroy it will be with this sword."

Chapter Eleven

The light in the forest was starting to turn a deeper golden colour as the afternoon wore on. The guardians had retreated, to confer over what plans needed to be made, and Caractacus had taken Simon and Cat to a small clearing nearby. At one end there was a shelter made of branches all bent over and twined together, interwoven with ivy and honeysuckle. Cat thought it was beautiful. Inside, the mossy floor was soft, and in front, where the shelter was open to the clearing, there was a crackling fire.

"You can sleep here," said Caractacus. "It's close to the Tree – probably the safest place in all the worlds right now. And just at the moment, yours is the only bit of deep amber we're sure of – we don't want to risk losing it to Ravenglass."

Cat put her hand up and fingered the jewel around her neck.

"Could he take it from me?" she said, curious. "When he tried, last time…" She remembered the fight, at Sunset Court, and the way she had held the amber and just told Lord Ravenglass and his henchmen to go back to where they came from. The power of the stone had pulled them instantly into a swirling white mist, all of them quite helpless to resist.

Caractacus shrugged.

"It's true," he said. "You could defend yourself with the amber if any one tried to take it directly from you. But you have to sleep, after all. You may be careless. You could be tricked."

Simon frowned. "But the amber's Cat's now," he objected. "She picked it up. Doesn't that make her the proper heir, or something?"

Caractacus waggled his tentacles at him. "Yes and no," he said. "Actually, any heir to the kingdom can take control of a piece of amber. But of course the one who is the current wielder is usually deemed to have the right to it. They can pass it on to whom they choose. In your case, your great-aunt wasn't able to pass the earth amber on, so it went to the first heir to take it. And that was Cat."

He seemed lost in thought for a moment, and then he shook himself. "We need to find the other bits of amber. Then maybe we can put an end to whatever foolishness Ravenglass has in his head, before he does more damage."

Simon mooched around the clearing, kicking the odd pile of leaves, feeling completely disgruntled. Here he was in a magic other world, and he may as well have been in the Forest of Dean on a camping holiday. Cat was deep in conversation with Caractacus about the Akkadian Empire and how it differed from the one on Earth all those years ago. She seemed quite happy to accept that they would be staying here, in the forest, till the last two pieces of amber had been found. But as far as Simon was concerned, that was no kind of adventure at all. How would he ever find out anything about Dad, or the place where he'd grown up, stuck here in the middle of the Great Forest? He wanted to see the rest of the kingdom, do some exploring.

He glanced at the two of them, heads bent over a tiny glowing replica of a city Caractacus had conjured on the forest floor. Cat looked up and raised her eyebrows, and Simon jerked his thumb into the main part of the forest. "Going for a walk!" he mouthed. She looked a little hesitant, but then nodded and turned back to Caractacus, asking him another question about portals. Simon watched them for a moment, and then slipped quietly away.

The forest seemed calmer than it had when they'd arrived. There were no odd sounds or surprising glimpses of other worlds. Late afternoon sunshine filtered down through the trees, dappling the path with showers of gold that danced and twinkled as Simon passed. There was the trill and chatter of birds, and occasionally Simon saw one or two flitting between branches, but they were quite normal-looking – nothing multi-coloured or exotic. He pushed his hands into his trouser pockets crossly.

As he did so, his fingers brushed against the hilt of the sword attached to his belt. He pulled it out of the makeshift strap he'd secured it with and held it out in front of him. Sunlight gleamed along its length and picked out the faint engravings on the blade. Simon took hold of the hilt with two hands and swung the sword through the air, left and then right. It made a satisfying swishing sound and took the tips off a few plants as it passed across them. Simon continued down the path, randomly cutting the heads off weeds and trimming bits of straggly undergrowth as he went, imagining himself a giant, scything down puny enemies with every swish of his sword. Until he came to a small, narrow path that led off the main one, dark with brambles, twisting into the depths of the forest.

On a whim, Simon turned and started following the little narrow footpath, and then another that led off that, and another, cutting his way through increasingly dense creepers and brambles with the sword. The paths wound in between the trees, darting in strange directions and then doubling back on themselves.

It wasn't long before he realised he was quite lost. The trees pressed around him, and the path he was following appeared to be getting ever narrower. But then he spotted a clearing, and a faint glimpse of something shining on the other side – a dim blueish-white gleam like the reflection of pale daylight on snow.

Simon approached the light, treading softly, the sword out in front of him. As he came closer, and the trees started to thin out, he saw that there was a rocky cliff rising ahead of him on the other side of the clearing, and at the base of the cliff was the outline of a dark cave, surrounded by ice and snow. Simon halted at the edge of the trees, scanning the cliff for signs of life. The snow and ice clearly didn't belong in the forest – it must be part of another world, one of those shifts that they had encountered on their way to the Great Tree. It would disappear in a moment.

But it didn't.

As Simon stood there, watching, there was a movement in the cave, and then a figure emerged. Simon couldn't see him clearly, but it was a man, he thought, tall and thin, dark-haired. The man stood for a while, in shadow, staring across the snow at the point where Simon was standing.

He can't see me, thought Simon. *He can't see me. I'm in another world.*

But the man stood quite still, gazing in Simon's direction. And then he moved out of the shadow, and as he did so, Simon blinked. There was something odd about the way the man changed as he moved out of the cave – a trick of the light, or something. Now he was nearer, Simon could see he was gaunt, pale, dressed in rags, and his hair was blond. His blue eyes were fixed on Simon's with an intent expression. And then they shifted to the sword at Simon's side.

He looked back at Simon and his eyes seemed to burn in his pale face.

"You are carrying my sword," he said.

His voice was rusty, as if he hadn't spoken for years. Simon stared at his prominent cheekbones, his ragged clothes, his bare feet on the snow. It was impossible that he was not shivering, frozen – but there was a kind of energy about him that seemed to be keeping him warm. Despite his obvious thinness, he gave the impression of a powerful strength, just held in check.

"Your sword?' said Simon. "But... I don't understand. Are you... are you Bruni?"

The man moved closer, and as he did so there was a clinking sound. Simon could see silver chains stretched out behind him, and sores on his arms and legs where the manacles were attached.

He beckoned Simon to come forward. Hesitantly, Simon moved from the shelter of the trees, but when he reached the point where the snow started he came up against an invisible barrier, separating him from the other world. The man moved towards him and then stopped, a few steps from the barrier, his chains almost stretched out to their full length.

"No, not Bruni," he said. "Bruni's sword was passed down to me. I am his heir. But how can you possibly…?"

He looked as if he were trying to remember something. And then, reaching out his hand till it was almost touching the barrier, he said, wonderingly: "Simon?"

Simon took a step backward, startled. How could this man know his name? Why was he claiming the sword was his? What was going on?

"W-what? Who…?" he stuttered, but inside him a great whirlwind of emotions was spiralling round. There was something about the man's eyes – that deep blue colour, like Cat's. It was bringing up memories Simon hadn't even realised he had – a voice, the touch of a hand on his shoulder, the feeling of being pulled close into a warm embrace.

"Dad?" he said. His voice was barely a whisper.

"Simon! It *is* you! I can't believe it! How can you be here? How can you be so *big*?"

The man had tears running down his face, and Simon could feel that his own eyes were streaming – he could hardly see the cave, the snow, the hand held out in front of him.

He blinked, brushed the tears away, and tried to grin.

"*Dad!* I knew you were alive. I *knew* it! I knew we'd find you! Wait till I tell Cat!"

Cat was seriously worried about where Simon had got to. Caractacus had left a while ago, claiming he had "important forest business to attend to", and she'd been waiting for Simon to return ever since. She kept wondering whether she should go and look for him – but he could have gone anywhere and more than likely they'd just end up following each other around in circles. So when he finally stumbled back into the clearing where they'd made camp, she wasn't sure whether to be relieved or furious at him for leaving in the first place. The sight of his face, though, pushed all thought of scolding out of her head.

"Simon! You look awful! What happened?"

Simon grinned. His face was covered in streaks from where he'd wiped tears away with muddy hands, and scratches from fighting his way through a pile of brambles on his way back to the clearing. His discovery had also left him looking slightly wild-eyed, with a mixture of shock, excitement and joy.

"Cat! I've found him!" he said. "Dad! He's alive! I *told* you!"

Cat stared at him in disbelief. "Simon! Are you insane? How? It *can't* have been... You've made a mistake."

"It's true – it really is! He's trapped in another world but... well, you know how weird the forest is, and then I think the sword must have had something to do with it, too – must have made the connection happen... It's him. Really – it's him!"

In his excitement he grabbed Cat by the shoulders and shook her, willing her to believe him. He could feel the tears prickling at the corners of his eyes again as he remembered seeing his dad, so pale and thin but so definitely alive.

"OK, OK, calm down," said Cat, patting him

on the shoulder. "Sit down and tell me everything – from the beginning."

It didn't take long. Simon's words tumbled out of his mouth with barely a breath to stop the flow, describing the cave, the man, the way he had recognised the sword, the way Simon had recognised him. And then at the end, he grew slightly more sober, and paused.

"Cat – he told me how to rescue him," he said. "We need the amber."

Cat didn't reply. She was still trying to get over the shock. Could it be true? Was Dad really alive – here, in the kingdom? Or had Simon got it wrong? He'd been very little when Dad died – how much did he really remember of him? She hugged her knees up towards her body, memories of her dad flooding into her mind – memories of strong arms and a deep voice, laughing blue eyes and the feeling of being lifted up and swung around. She suddenly found herself biting her thumb – something she hadn't done for years.

"Cat," said Simon again. "He told me something very important. We need to leave the forest. We can't tell anyone else about him or where we're going."

Cat focused on him and frowned.

"Leave the forest?' she said.

"Yes," said Simon, lowering his voice. "He said we can get him out of where he's trapped, but we need the amber and the sword. And we have to go to the palace to do it."

"But we can't! That's where Lord Ravenglass is. He'll catch us for sure – and then he'll have the amber *and* the sword. It's madness!"

"I know – but it has to be the palace. He said it's the only place in this world where there's a proper link to his prison."

"But you saw him here, in the forest. Can't we reach him from here?"

Simon shook his head impatiently. "No – we could see each other, and talk, but he said it's not a real link – just something to do with the sword, and the magic of the forest. If we want to reach him – release him – we have to go to the palace. And there's another thing."

Simon looked round, to check no one was near, and then put his face very close to Cat's. His voice was low, but determined.

"They'll try to stop us – Caractacus and the forest people. That's what he said. We've got to go, Cat – we've got to! He told me a secret way into the palace. He told me where to go. If we're quick and careful, he said, we won't get caught by Lord Ravenglass. But we mustn't tell anyone. We can't trust Caractacus!"

Cat looked at his eager face and hesitated. She felt utterly confused. Caractacus was odd, certainly, but she had warmed to the strange blue creature since he'd burst into Simon's bedroom that morning. He had the same sort of reassuring presence as the previous forest agent they'd met – Albert Jemmet. But then she thought about the odd expression on her mum's face when she'd first seen Caractacus – the hint of recognition, of fear. Was Simon right? Was Caractacus not to be trusted?

"Simon – I don't know. But I don't think we should leave the forest. It's dangerous."

Simon groaned in frustration. "But this is *Dad* we're talking about," he said, pleading with her. "I saw him, he knew who I was! And he's so thin, and he's got these chains keeping him trapped in the ice. We can *rescue* him, Cat. Don't you think we have to try?"

Cat took a deep breath.

"I think, before we decide anything, you'd better take me to the place where you saw Dad. If it *is* Dad. I need to see him for myself. And then we'll decide."

Chapter Twelve

Simon managed to find the cave again, but it was almost dusk by the time they reached the clearing, and the place where Gwyn Arnold was trapped seemed to be only half there, as if it was fading away. Still, Cat could just see the man standing by the cliff face, silver chains stretching out from his arms and legs. She walked with hesitation towards the barrier, and saw him move across the ice and snow to meet her. There was a lump in her throat as she saw the sores on his skin.

"Dad?" she said.

"Catrin," he replied. Tears were glistening on his cheeks but he was smiling, his hand reached out to touch the invisible barrier between them.

He looked older, his face gaunt, but it was definitely Dad. She wanted to cry, and hug him.

"The link is fading," he said, as the ice around him started to shimmer. "You need to get to the palace. Please – Simon knows where to go. You can get me out of here, *but you mustn't tell anyone from the forest*. They can't know you've seen me."

Cat nodded, dumbly, and held out her hand – but he'd already gone. Trees crowded in where the ice and snow had been. Cat was left stunned. Tears of joy that he was alive mingled with an awful feeling of loss as his image faded.

She and Simon hurried back to the shelter and gathered their bags. Quickly and quietly they slipped away through the trees into the gathering dusk.

Getting out of the Great Forest, however, proved to be an almost impossible task. Whatever path they took just seemed to lead round in circles – and leaving the path and trying to push through the trees and undergrowth was worse. It was as if the trees *moved*, thought Cat. As if they were herding them back towards the centre.

After an hour or more of slogging through brambles and following twisting tracks that never seemed to go anywhere, Cat gave up, flung her backpack on the ground, and sat on it firmly.

"This is ridiculous," she said. "We're never going to get out."

Simon slumped down next to her.

"You're right. I'm sure we've been down this path twice already."

"If not three times," said Cat. She thought about what Dad had said, about not trusting the forest agents. Did that mean not trusting the tree guardians, too? Could their magic be preventing her and Simon from leaving?

She shook her head, trying to clear her mind, and glanced round at the trees. "We need to find some way to break the power of the forest. I'm sure it's trying to keep us here..."

Simon stood up, and as he did so there was a faint call from a long way behind them.

"Simon! Cat! Come back! What do you think you're doing?"

They looked at each other.

"It's Caractacus!" said Simon. "Run!"

Cat grabbed her backpack and slung it over her shoulder, and they pelted into a gap between the trees, twisted round a huge oak and half slid, half ran down a muddy slope. At the bottom, Simon hesitated, then slipped sideways between two thorny brambles and along what looked like a dried-up stream bed. Cat followed, stumbling on the stony ground and having to duck as trailing brambles and wayward branches whipped across in front of her. It felt as if they were alive, catching in her hair and her clothes, pulling her back. She could hear Caractacus shouting after them, his voice closer now.

"Simon! Cat! It's dangerous! You mustn't leave!"

Cat put on a burst of speed and caught up with Simon just as he reached the end of the little stream bed they were in. They both stopped, shocked. At their feet the ground fell away steeply, narrowing far below them into a rocky valley, while on either side dense thorny bushes closed in. The only way out was back the way they had come, and that was the direction from which Caractacus was coming.

"It's the forest," said Simon, panting. "It's got us trapped."

Cat bent over and held her knees, catching her breath. "I think – I think I know what to do," she gasped. "The amber…"

"Of course!" said Simon. "Genius! It can take us anywhere! Quick – Cat, get it!"

Cat reached up and pulled the amber jewel out from where it had been tucked inside her jumper. She could feel it, slightly warm, glowing between her fingers, but she had no idea whether she could make it work. "Albert said you just have to tell it where to go – but we probably have to be quite specific. And I don't know where in the palace we're meant to be going."

"The south-west tower," said Simon instantly. "Dad told me. There's a drain, and you can creep up it into the castle cellars. That's where there's the connection to his prison."

They could hear a crashing noise behind them now. It was almost certainly Caractacus, and he was very close.

"Cat – quick!" said Simon, grabbing her hand. "Now!"

Cat held the amber firmly, and tried to focus on the power she knew was in the jewel. "We want to go to the south-west tower of Queen Igraine's palace, where the drain comes out," she gabbled, feeling a little foolish. She could hear Caracatus fluttering out of the trees behind her, shouting, and she thought they had probably failed. They were going to be caught.

But then she gasped, because she felt as if she'd been immersed in cold water. The trees all around them disappeared in a kaleidoscope of colours and shapes, and the next second, the whirling shapes around her resolved into grey stone walls and hard ground, and there was the unmistakeable smell of sewers.

Next to her, Simon was on his hands and knees being sick onto the cobblestones. Cat felt slightly queasy herself, but being the one holding the amber seemed to have saved her from the worst of it. She knelt down by Simon and put her hand on his shoulder.

"Are you all right?"

He spat, wiped his mouth on his sleeve and sat up, his skin tinged green.

"That was *awesome!*" he said, and grinned. She rolled her eyes, and then looked around them.

They were in some kind of narrow alley, with grey stone walls stretching up on both sides. To their left, the wall continued up and then became a tall white tower – to their right, they could see a jumble of roofs. Most of the width of the alley was taken up with a deep open channel, with grey water running down it, and leaves and twigs and some things Cat didn't want to think about swirling around in the flow. The channel led all the way up to a dark archway cut into the stone wall of the tower. The cobbled path they were standing on accompanied it to the wall and then stopped – after that, the only way forward was to wade upstream, through the archway and into the palace drains.

"Uurgh," said Cat, looking at the water.

Simon shrugged. "It's fine – come on. Dad said you only had to wade for a short section."

Cat made a face and started to take off her trainers and socks and roll up her trousers. The drain was about half a metre deep and she'd almost certainly end up with wet jeans, but at least she'd have something dry to put on her feet when they got to the other end. If they ever did. Trying not to look at the bits floating past her, she eased one foot gingerly into the swirling grey water and took her first step up the drain.

Chapter Thirteen

Once she got over her disgust, the palace drain proved easier to negotiate than Cat had expected. It wasn't long before they found the small, secret door Dad had told Simon about, and it opened exactly as it was supposed to, into the cellars. Simon led them confidently through a series of small storage chambers and then down two flights of stairs, but at that point he slowed, less sure of himself. He took a left turn, and then another.

"How much further on do we have to go?" said Cat, as they reached a divide.

"Until we get to where we need to be," said Simon shortly. He was feeling responsible for finding the right place and unsure whether he'd properly remembered the instructions for how to get there. Besides, there was something nagging at the back of his brain, a small voice that wondered if he hadn't, after all, made a terrible mistake. Was it madness, walking into the palace like this? Were they really going to be able to rescue Dad from his icy prison? He tried to push the voice away. Whatever they were risking, it had to be done. They had to try.

"I think it's this way," he said, gesturing to the right this time, and sounding altogether more confident than he felt. They set off along the corridor and at the end, to Simon's immense relief, they found a spiral staircase, going down. Seeping up the stairwell, from the chamber below, was a very pale blueish light.

"That's it!" said Simon. "It's down there!"

He looked at Cat, her face just faintly visible in the reflected light. She was holding the amber protectively, and Simon found his own hand moving to the hilt of the sword tucked into his belt. She nodded, and they started to descend the stairs.

As they did so, the light got stronger, and when they got to the bottom they could see the outline of an arched doorway leading into another chamber. The blueish light was coming from beyond the arch. Simon felt Cat take hold of his arm. As they emerged into the chamber, they could see that the stone floor ended only a few metres from the doorway, and beyond that was snow and ice and the dark outline of a cave.

"Dad?" called Simon softly. "Dad – we're here!"

"Excellent," came a voice from the shadows behind them – but it wasn't the voice of their father.

Simon felt as if his feet had been glued to the ground. He recognised the voice. It was the very last one he'd been hoping to hear. It was the voice of Lord Ravenglass.

"Took you rather longer than I expected," drawled the voice, and then Lord Ravenglass himself emerged from behind them, shaking out his lace cuffs and pushing a stray curl of black hair from his face with an elegant white finger. "But better late than never, as they say."

He held out his hand to Cat, who appeared to be frozen, and touched her lightly on the shoulder.

"Welcome to my palace," he said, and then turned to Simon. He smiled, his white teeth gleaming, his long face lit up with pleasure, the rings on his fingers sparkling in the cold bright light of the chamber.

"My dears," he said. "So good of you to come to help us. *Just* what your dear father and I were hoping you'd do."

Lord Ravenglass gestured into the chamber, to the line of ice and snow that started halfway across the floor. The gaunt figure of Gwyn Arnold was standing just beyond the barrier, smiling at them. Ravenglass laid his hand gently on Simon's head, and Simon felt as if he'd been wrapped in a warm blanket. He could move again, and the cold dread that he'd felt when he first heard Lord Ravenglass's voice melted away as if it had never been. A sense of relief came over him, a sense that it was all going to be all right. Lord Ravenglass was on their side – he would *help* rescue their dad. They were in exactly the right place and with exactly the right person.

Cat was puzzled. She felt she ought to be worried by the presence of Lord Ravenglass, but oddly it didn't seem to bother her. She looked across at the man standing on the other side of the cellar, in the snow and ice. He was very still, his eyes on her and Simon, his expression hard to read.

Cat moved forward till she was prevented by what felt like a wall of solid air. She put her hand up against the barrier. On the other side, the man moved towards her and delicately touched the edge of his world with his fingertips. Their hands appeared to be only a small distance apart, but Cat could not reach across the gap to touch him.

"Dad!" she said. She could see him so much more clearly now. As she looked at the deep lines in his pale face, his ragged clothes and matted hair, she felt a twist in her stomach.

He smiled. "It's me, Catrin. I'm here, in the cellar… or rather, part of my world is here. Where I am – this prison – it touches a part of every world. But you can't reach me fully. No one can come here without the power to travel to all the worlds at once."

Simon came over, his voice eager. "But how did you end up there? And how do we release you?"

For a moment the man's face tightened, in pain or anger, Cat wasn't sure. He almost looked like a different person. And then he relaxed, and he was their father again – Gwyn Arnold, the man they'd always been told had died in a car crash.

"I was betrayed," Gwyn said. "I was imprisoned here, using all the power the forest could muster."

"Betrayed?" said Cat. "Who betrayed you?"

Gwyn looked across at her, his expression bleak, his voice full of pain. "Lou," he said. "I thought he was my friend. But I was wrong. The forest was trying to gain complete power over all the worlds and I was trying to stop them. I thought Lou was, too." He punched the barrier with his fist and his voice cracked as he gave a great shout of rage and frustration. "Lou sold me to the forest, and they imprisoned me here. Only Ravenglass stayed loyal to me."

Cat and Simon looked at each other, shocked.

"*Uncle Lou?*" said Cat, in disbelief. For a moment she felt utterly bewildered. But then she felt Ravenglass's reassuring hand on her shoulder and she realised that it made total sense. Uncle Lou was one of the forest agents – they called him the Druid. He was Dad's cousin, and for a while he'd helped bring Cat and Simon up after Gwyn had died. But he must have just been trying to keep an eye on them, make sure no one suspected he'd been responsible for Gwyn's 'death'. She caught her breath.

"Simon! That's what the row must have been about! Mum and Uncle Lou! When she made him leave… She must have realised he'd had something to do with Dad's death!"

"Undoubtedly so," said the smooth voice of Lord Ravenglass behind them. "An astute woman, your mother. You would do well to follow her lead as far as the Druid is concerned."

He moved closer, and put a fatherly hand on each of their shoulders.

"My dears," he said gently. "It's been quite a shock for you. To realise you've been on the wrong side all this time."

Simon nodded slowly, as if trying to take it all in. Then he pulled out the sword from his belt and held it out in front of Gwyn.

"This is yours, then," he said. "Mum said it was yours. But it's made from parts of all the worlds. Could we use it to get to where you are?"

Gwyn shook his head regretfully. "It's not powerful enough on its own. But it's good you have it, Simon. I'm gad you have my sword." His expression softened. "Perhaps Ravenglass can teach you to use it. And when I'm released, I'll give you a few lessons myself. What do you say?"

"I'd – I'd like that," said Simon. "Very much."

Cat reached out and squeezed Simon's hand. She took hold of the bronze chain round her neck and drew it over her head, holding the glowing amber jewel in front of her. She watched the flecks and whorls of orange and brown at its heart, moving ceaselessly. Then she took a deep breath and held it up to Lord Ravenglass.

"Use it," she said. "Whatever you need to do. Use it to release him."

Lord Ravenglass held out his elegant white hand and Cat dropped the amber into it. He stared down at it for a moment, his expression unreadable. Then his long white fingers closed over the jewel and he slipped it into one of the pockets of his rich velvet coat.

He smiled at them both. "Excellent. Excellent. But one is not enough. I'm afraid we need all four to release your father. Only the amber crown can dissolve his prison. If we can find the other two before the forest puts them out of reach, then I will have enough power to take the final amber from the queen. And then... we can release your father."

He beckoned to the two children, and gestured up the stairs out of the cellar. "Come, my dears. Your father's not going anywhere just yet. You need to rest, and we need to make plans. Only a few hours ago I was informed that my accomplices have located one of the missing bits of amber. In Akkadia. They may in fact have it in their grasp as we speak." He rubbed his hands happily. "Things are going our way, I do believe. Things are finally going our way."

PART FIVE

Chapter Fourteen

The headquarters of the Most Illustrious Company of the Thieves of Ur was a veritable treasure house of old documents, ancient maps and guides to the more obscure secret passages that riddled the city of Ur-Akkad. The entrance was a small obscure cave in the hills to the south of the city – no one entering it would ever know that behind an apparently solid rock-face was a whole set of interconnecting caverns furnished with every luxury and stocked with enough food and drink to last a hundred years of siege. But here the Thieves had kept their most treasured possessions for generations, and here secret information on every building in the city was to be found. It had taken the Druid most of the day to find the map he needed, but now it was in his hands – the map that revealed the layout of the labyrinth under the Sargon's palace.

"There!" he said, putting his finger on the central chamber right at the heart of the labyrinth. "It will be there – I'm sure of it."

Nasir Hunzu, Lord Commander of the Thieves of Ur, pulled at his square beard thoughtfully.

"The labyrinth is somewhere we avoid, my friend," he said. "You know the rumours – it's said that deep in the heart of the labyrinth the empire has a source of mighty power. It's what they have used to subdue and capture magic for generations. Every man who has tried to find that source of power has died." He leant over the Druid and said, with low emphasis, "There are *dragons* in that labyrinth."

The Druid shrugged, and gave Nasir a wry grin. "I know. But I need that source of power – it's what I came for. So I'll just have to take my chances." He clapped Nasir on the back. "You don't need to risk any of the thieves," he said cheerfully. "The map is what I needed. I can go alone."

Nasir frowned at him. "The Thieves of Ur are their own masters," he said. "They will come or not as they please. But *I* shall come with you."

He grinned, revealing a fine set of teeth stained reddish-brown with betel nut juice. "If we can steal the dragon's stone, the heart of the empire, the fame of the Thieves will last forever!"

The Druid sighed. "If we manage to steal the dragon amber, then Ur-Akkad might just survive, along with all the other worlds. If we don't, Nasir, there may be no one to remember the Thieves of Ur at all."

Nasir laughed, and clapped the Druid on the back. "You are too gloomy, my friend. Come, we will drink to the endeavour, and then we will set off. There is an entrance to the labyrinth just off the Kallaba Canal, a little downstream of the temple. We can be there in less time than it takes to drink a good bottle of Sumerian wine."

As he ushered the Druid towards a low table set with pastries and goblets, he caught the eye of a thin man with a straggly beard, leaning against the wall nearby. Unseen by the Druid, Nasir made a slight gesture with his hand, and the man nodded and slipped away into the shadows.

The entrance to the labyrinth off the Kallaba Canal was less of an entrance and more of an accident. Water seepage had caused subsidence and one wall of the tunnel had collapsed. Because it had happened in rather an out-of-the-way corner of the labyrinth, Nasir said, no one had yet seen fit to repair it.

The Druid clambered over the rubble that half obscured the entrance and stuck his head into the labyrinth.

"It seems deserted," he said, turning back to his companions. "Shall we?"

Rahul, wiping the sweat from his forehead with the tail end of his shirt and glancing nervously behind him, nodded. Nasir gestured to Ishmel to follow, and then climbed across the rubble after him. As they all clambered down into the darkness, the Druid conjured a werelight and they looked around them in wonder.

The passage was well built and long. It disappeared into shadow in both directions with no apparent turns. On the walls, faded murals of dragons and other fabulous beasts were interspersed with scenes from the history of the Akkadian Empire, and portraits of some of the ninety-eight Sargons that had preceded the present one.

"This isn't an obscure corner," said the Druid, looking at the images with a frown. "This is the central passage. We must be not very far from –"

"The guard room," finished Nasir. "Just so."

As he spoke, there was a tramp of feet, and from each end of the corridor twenty or more imperial guards appeared, shields up, spears at the ready.

Nasir shrugged. "I'm sorry, my friend," he said. "The Ensi paid in gold…"

Rahul looked round wildly. "You – you *sold* us?" he squeaked in outrage. "You sold our friend? You sold the honour of the Thieves… to *Ra-Kaleel*?"

He launched himself at Nasir, but the commander stepped backwards and twisted out of reach, wagging his finger at the red-faced Rahul. "The honour of the Thieves, Rahul?" he said. "Our honour is money – we thieve for the one who pays the most. Remember?"

"But we do *not* betray our friends!" said Ishmel angrily, his foot shooting out to kick Nasir on the shin. Nasir stumbled, and then the guards at either end of the corridor gave a shout, and suddenly Ishmel, Rahul and the Druid found themselves fighting back to back against an assault from both directions, while Nasir slipped quietly behind the line of guards and out of the labyrinth.

It wasn't a long fight. Despite the Druid taking out a fair few assailants with some well-directed immobility spells and Rahul's surprising agility for a man of his bulk, they were heavily outnumbered. Soon all three were disarmed, bound and gagged.

"Orders, sir?" said one of the guards, who had just finished securing the Druid's wrists. "Where do we take them?"

The captain, surveying the carnage around him, frowned. "To the fires of the afterlife for all I care. But I believe the Chief Ensi wants the tall one. Take him to the central chamber. You can leave the other two tied up for the dragons."

Chapter Fifteen

Jem, Dora and Inanna were deep in the Akkadian labyrinth. If it wasn't for Dora's werelight they would have had no chance of navigating the dark winding tunnels. Even with it, they were beginning to lose heart. Jem was convinced they'd been down the same side tunnel twice now, and there seemed no way to tell if they were closer to the palace or further away from it. The tunnels all looked the same – square-cut marble walls and a flat, even stone floor stretching on ahead of them into the darkness.

After about half an hour of feeling their way along, trying to guess which fork to take when the tunnel divided, trying to remember how many left turns and how many right turns they'd taken, Jem halted by yet another side passage and threw himself to the ground with a groan.

"This is hopeless! We'll never find our way to the dragon's heart or wherever we're supposed to be going! We need some kind of map – without one it's just guesswork!"

Inanna sat down next to him and leant her head on his shoulder. "My feet hurt," she said. "I'm fed up of just walking and walking. Maybe we should give up on your amber stone. Maybe you could just take me to your world, Jem?"

She gazed up at him with pleading brown eyes, and Jem wondered whether to put his arm around her, give her an encouraging hug. But then he looked at Dora and saw her expression. He hurriedly shifted Inanna away from his shoulder.

"We can't take you back without finding the Druid first," he said firmly. "We need to get through these tunnels. Come on, Inanna – you've known the temple labyrinth all your life… Isn't there *anything* we could use to guide us?"

Inanna pulled her knees up to her chest and looked sulky. "It's quite different down here from in the temple. For one thing, the tunnels are much deeper. And the signs make no sense."

"What signs?" said Dora. "We haven't seen any signs."

"On the walls. Wherever there's a divide or turning," said Inanna. "Small carvings – didn't you notice them?"

She pointed to a smoother part of the wall, just near the side passage, and Dora held up her werelight and peered at it.

"Jem!" she said. "It's a spell sign! It's one of the ones that were on Simon and Catrin's box – the box with the other bit of amber."

Jem jumped to his feet and bent over next to Dora. She was right. Carved faintly into the wall, so faintly that they'd not noticed till now, was a triangle with lines and squiggles inside. He frowned at Inanna. "You should have told us about these before!"

"I'm sorry," she said. "But they just didn't make any sense to me. The signs in the temple labyrinth tell you where to go – these are just strange shapes and lines."

"They're spells," said Dora. "This one's for a fiery wind. They're associated with the amber somehow. Maybe if we follow it we'll finally start going in the right direction."

The fire symbols led them rapidly to a series of passages that were taller and wider, lined with well-cut pale stones. The floor sloped and they appeared to be descending deeper underground, but to Jem's surprise the air was getting warmer, not colder. There were strange noises now, too – faint sounds from far away echoing down the passages. After one particularly loud one, Dora stopped.

"Did that… did that sound to you like – ?" she shivered.

"Yes," said Jem grimly. "A dragon's cry. A long way away, though."

Inanna clutched Jem tightly on the arm. "Really?" she breathed. "Really dragons? In the passages?"

He nodded. "There's a smell of them, too," he said. "They've got a lair somewhere near. When I hatched those baby dragons in the castle last year, the stables stank just like this. But if we stay quiet, and keep out of their way, we should be all right."

They crept down the next few passages, keeping an anxious ear out, but the dragons didn't seem to be getting any closer. Finally they reached the end of a long passage and came to a dead halt in front of a flat wall. Carved in the middle of the wall was the fire spell, alongside two other symbols, each a kind of triangle with other signs carved inside them.

"It's the opening spell that was on Simon and Catrin's box," said Dora.

"Well, say the spell then!" said Jem eagerly.

"It's a very powerful spell," said Dora. "We have no idea what we're opening. Anything could happen!"

Jem gave her an encouraging clap on the back. "It'll be fine," he said confidently. "Honestly, Dora, you're always so cautious. If the signs call for an opening spell, then we need to conjure an opening spell. And you'd better get on with it, before the dragons find us!"

Dora gave him a hard stare, then raised her arms and said the words of the spell.

A sheet of flame leapt up in front of them, and then seemed to melt into the wall, which turned white and started to crackle with frost. The next second a tornado whipped around them, pulling at their clothes and hair and almost knocking them off their feet. As it died down, a crack appeared in the stone in front of them, and then a door flew open, revealing a large cavern lit with a dim orange glow. As they stepped inside there was an ear-splitting roar. Flames billowed out of the shadows, and then a dark shape emerged, hurtling across the cavern straight towards them. It was an enormous red dragon, fire and smoke spewing from its massive jaws.

Dora, Jem and Inanna threw themselves backwards, and as the dragon reached the doorway, they scuttled sideways and flattened themselves against the outer wall. They were just out of sight of the dragon's questing nose pushing through the doorway next to them, but there was no way of getting back down the corridor without passing within reach of its gleaming pointed teeth. Dora tried very hard not to make a sound, but Inanna kept giving faint whimpers of fear and Dora was finding it hard to control her breathing. Only Jem seemed relatively calm. He was studying the end of the dragon's nose with interest.

"Dora?" he whispered. "It's a red dragon. Like the one at home. I think I can make friends with it."

"Make friends?" she mouthed back. "Have you finally lost your wits, Jem? How exactly are you going to make friends with a dragon?"

"I've got some cob nuts in my pocket," he said, bending close to her ear. "Those baby dragons I hatched – they all loved cob nuts. If I offered this one some, we might be able to get her to let us in. Dragons are quite sweet when you're not threatening them!"

It was true, thought Dora – the baby dragons *had* loved cob nuts. And Jem did have a way with animals. But on the other hand, he'd reared those dragons from hatchlings. This was a fully grown dragon – and so far, it hadn't been very friendly.

Dora hesitated, then nodded. "All right – try. But be *really* careful, Jem. Don't go in there unless you're certain!"

Jem gave her a thumb's up. He reached into his pocket and came out with a handful of slightly grimy nuts which he rubbed a little cleaner on his jerkin. Then he peeled himself from the wall and started to move towards the dragon, making soothing noises as he did so. Dora held her breath.

As Jem approached, the dragon snorted and moved backwards a little. Jem balanced a cob nut on the flat of his hand and held it out, continuing to make soothing noises as he moved forward. The dragon withdrew its nose from the doorway, and Jem walked slowly into the chamber beyond, still holding out the cob nut and making little clicks with his tongue.

Dora looked across at Inanna, and the two of them moved away from the wall and peered into the doorway to see what was happening.

The dragon was sitting back on its haunches, watching Jem with one fierce green eye, its head cocked slightly. Jem continued to croon at it, holding up the cob nut.

"Nice cob nut, lovely cob nut, your favourite – yum yum, crunchy, delicious, can't you smell them…?"

The dragon snorted again, and then slowly lowered its head to the same level as Jem's. It gazed at him with a rather baleful expression. Jem's voice started to get a hint of desperation.

"Come on now, there's a good beast – have a lovely yummy cob nut from Uncle Jem, why don't you?"

He held out the nut again.

There was a tense pause and Dora wanted

to shout at Jem to run – but her voice wouldn't work. The dragon started to open its mouth and Dora shut her eyes. She couldn't bear to watch. But a moment later she heard Inanna gasp and clap her hands, and she opened her eyes to see the dragon delicately curling its tongue round the cob nut on Jem's palm. It placed the nut in its mouth and crunched it experimentally. As it did so, Jem reached up and scratched the dragon on the nose just between its two nostrils. The dragon shivered with pleasure and put out its tongue to lick Jem's face.

"Jem! You did it! You are *so* brave!" squealed Inanna, and she danced into the chamber clapping her hands.

Jem looked up, wiped the dragon slime from his face with the back of his sleeve, and grinned.

"It's a sweetie," he said. "Just an old softie. Aren't you, my lovely?" He scratched the dragon's nose again and offered it another couple of cob nuts.

Dora walked carefully into the chamber. Her legs were only just starting to feel like they belonged to her again.

"Well done," she said, rather shakily, and Jem,

after a swift look at her white face, patted her comfortingly on the shoulder.

"I knew I could do it. You needn't have worried," he said, and gave her plaits a friendly tug. "Come on. Let's find this fire amber then."

The huge chamber was mostly in shadow, but in the centre was what appeared to be some kind of large egg on a low pillar. Tendrils were snaking away from it into deep channels in the floor, and it was lit up with an eerie yellow-orange glow.

As the children moved towards it, the dragon followed, nudging Jem with her nose every now and again for a scratch. But just before they reached the pillar, three figures emerged from the shadows on the other side.

In the centre stood a tall man in white robes, with a square black beard and a heavy gold chain of office.

"Ra-Kaleel!" Inanna gasped.

But it was the two figures either side of him that made Jem and Dora turn cold. Two thin, dark-suited men with bright black eyes. Mr Smith and Mr Jones.

Chapter Sixteen

Mr Jones reached out one hand and intoned a few words. Dora, Jem and Inanna froze, expressions of shock still on their faces. He cocked his head and regarded them with a quizzical expression.

"Weren't those two –?"

"Yes," said Mr Smith. "They were there when we found the other piece of amber. The meddlesome young witch immobilised us, as I recall."

The corner of Mr Jones's mouth twitched briefly. "Then it's a case of biter bit, I do believe, Mr Smith."

He turned his attention to the odd tracery of green tendrils snaking in towards the object on the pillar in front of them. The tracery became more dense as it reached the centre, where it merged with an oval container of the same shiny, scaly material that the tendrils were made of.

He raised one eyebrow at Ra-Kaleel.

"Dragon hide," said the Chief Ensi in a rather tremulous voice. "The dragon hide contains the amber and draws power from it. Dragons are highly magical creatures, after all. The power is conducted from here along these channels you see in the floor – and then used to extract and contain magic from the prisoners in the cells beneath us."

"Ingenious," said Mr Smith, his eyes following the snaking ropes of dragon hide away from the centre of the chamber. "Channelling unruly magic for the good of the empire."

"Exactly," said Ra-Kaleel eagerly. "Exactly. And if you take the dragon amber, the whole magical grid will collapse. Our chariots, our spycopters, our light and power, our weapons – we can't survive without them! It will be chaos!"

Mr Smith grinned. "You are mistaking us," he said, and leant closer to Ra-Kaleel, "for people who give a damn. Now, how do we open this container?"

The Chief Ensi blanched. "Only obsidian…" he said faintly.

"What?" said Mr Jones, his eyes narrowing.

"*Only obsidian, cuts through the skin…* as the poem has it. We need obsidian blades."

"And you didn't tell us this before we came down here?" murmured Mr Smith, raising his eyes to the ceiling.

"Tut, tut," said Mr Jones.

The two men fixed him with their dark stares and the Chief Ensi's legs folded beneath him. He slumped to the floor, gibbering with fear. Dora, even immobilised, could feel the cold power that came from the two black-suited figures – an ancient malevolence that had nothing human in it.

Luckily for the Chief Ensi, there was a commotion at the other end of the chamber that drew Smith and Jones's attention away from him. Four members of the imperial guard were making their way out of the shadows, and between them was a rather battered and bloody figure, gagged, with his arms bound. The sight of him made Dora want to shout for joy and at the same time groan in despair. It was the Druid.

"Excellent," said Mr Jones in his rasping voice, as he surveyed the newcomers. "A reunion of old friends."

The Druid's brown eyes met Mr Jones's black ones steadily, but his expression was bleak. Switching his gaze to the dragon-hide container, he caught sight of Dora and Jem, standing like statues on the other side of the pillar, and his eyes brightened. He raised his bound hands in an attempt at a wave and nodded appreciatively at the dragon, who was nuzzling Jem's immobilised neck.

Mr Jones followed his gaze.

"The boy – he's got a knife," he rasped. "It seems they came better prepared than we did."

He gestured to Mr Smith, and the two of them circled round the pillar and made for Jem. Mr Smith had one hand on Jem's shoulder and Mr Jones was pulling at the knife tucked into Jem's belt when the dragon decided to intervene. She wasn't at all happy about these dark creatures mauling her new friend. Snorting imperiously, she gave Mr Jones a whack with one great, clawed foot, and then bit Mr Smith's arm.

Mr Jones went flying and Mr Smith gave

a great yowl of pain and anger. The dragon launched herself after them both, but before she did, she blew some steamy breath over Jem and then did the same for Dora and Inanna. Instantly they found the immobility spell had been lifted, and they could move.

Jem lost no time. He leapt towards the dragon-hide egg and slashed into it with his blade. The obsidian cut through the skin cleanly and the two halves fell away. Lying on the pillar was a round amber stone, with a heavy golden clasp. The amber burned with a fierce orange-yellow light and, deep inside it, twisting tongues of white fire seemed to move ceaselessly, their light reflecting off the gold chain lying pooled around the jewel.

Dora thought that she had never seen anything so beautiful, not even the piece of amber Cat had claimed in that other world where they'd last met Smith and Jones. But she couldn't stop to admire it – the two crow men were already on their feet and the guards had run to help them. The dragon was in retreat from their swords and a maelstrom of spells.

"Take the jewel but don't touch it – it will be

hot!" she shouted at Inanna, and rapidly threw an unbinding spell at the Druid.

Inanna hesitated, then wrapped the edge of her cloak around her hand and reached out for the gold chain. As she removed the jewel from its place, the glow of the amber started to fade, and the tendrils of dragon hide snaking away from the pillar darkened and started to shrivel.

"*No-o-o-o*...!" wailed Ra-Kaleel from the floor, clutching at the length of dragon hide nearest him. "You've ripped out the heart of the empire! You've destroyed us all! Our chariots, our city, our armies! You've broken the power of Ur-Akkad!"

The dragon gave a great roar and gouts of flame licked around the walls. A deep rumbling sound began to build and answering cries echoed faintly around the chamber.

"The other dragons!" said the Druid urgently. "They know the amber's been stolen!"

He gave a quick glance over his shoulder at the two crow men, still fighting off Jem's dragon, then sprinted forward, grabbing Dora's hand.

"Quickly!" he said. "Smith and Jones are keeping this one busy, for now, but the others won't take long to get here. We've got to get away!"

Jem and Inanna ran for the entrance they'd come in at, and the Druid and Dora followed. As they passed through the doorway there was a great roar from the dragon behind them, and spouts of flame scorched across the chamber, but Dora could see that Smith and Jones had pinned the dragon down with a binding spell, and they were now two dark shadows streaking impossibly fast towards the Druid and his companions.

"Closing spell, Dora!" yelled the Druid, as he held his arms out towards Smith and Jones and conjured a storm of magic to slow them down. Dora, breathing hard, mentally reversed the spell that had been carved on the wall and focused all her energy. She rapidly declaimed the words and hoped she hadn't made a mistake. Smith and Jones were wading forward against the hail of spells from the Druid. They were almost at the entrance when Dora's magic took hold, and the great stone doors slammed shut.

Dora breathed a huge sigh of relief – but then she heard Inanna cry out in shock, and she turned to see the Druid stagger. One of the crow men had managed to get a spell through the door just as it closed, and the Druid's left arm was now hanging uselessly at his side, while a great stain of blood was spreading rapidly across his chest.

"It's all right," he said, clutching on to Jem and grimacing. "I can walk. It looks worse than it is. If I can just lean on you, Jem…"

Together they stumbled down the long corridor. From behind them there was the sound of rock splitting and the ground was trembling as if there was an earthquake.

"They'll be through that door in a few minutes," said the Druid in a faint voice, his breathing ragged. "We need to hurry!"

"But where are we *going*?" said Inanna, panicking as they reached the end of the corridor. "I can hear more dragons – and they sound like they're *everywhere*!"

They stood, hesitating. Inanna was right – they could hear roars from every direction, and crashing sounds, as several huge, maddened dragons pounded through the labyrinth. Worse, from behind them was the sound of a different kind of cry – harsher, more rasping – and the beat of a multitude of wings.

"Smith and Jones!" cried Dora, her hand to her mouth. "They've got the door open. They've sent the crows after us!"

"Crows?" said Inanna, trembling.

"They're crow men," said Dora. "They can conjure hundreds of crows to attack us! Jem – we've got to get away!"

There was panic in her voice as she remembered the last time they'd fought Smith and Jones – the swarm of birds, the jabbing beaks and raking claws.

"This way!" said Jem. "Quick!"

He ushered them down the left-hand passage, dragging the Druid with him, and then cursed.

A large red dragon was crouching in the middle of the passageway, its fierce amber eyes fixed on them, its long tail curling up behind its great glittering body and lashing slowly from side to side.

"Damn," said the Druid, in a hoarse voice. He tried to throw a spell at it, but his face was very pale, and the dragon barely seemed to notice as the spell hit. It snorted, and slowly started to move towards them. At the same time, a tall, dark figure emerged from the passage they'd just left, a figure surrounded by a whirling mass of dark birds crying out in harsh voices.

I'll have to fight them, thought Dora. The blood seemed to have left every part of her body, and she could barely feel her fingers, but she knew she was the only one who could even try. The Druid was too weak and Inanna too inexperienced. She made a huge effort to stand up straight.

"Get behind me!" she said to the others urgently, then turned to face Mr Smith – or was it Mr Jones? – and started to gather her magic. But there was a commotion behind her, and muffled shouts, and then she felt her plaits being tugged. She was dragged, half falling, through a door that had just opened in the passage wall. As she stumbled onto her knees, she heard the heavy door slam behind her, and she looked up to see a bulky man with a richly embroidered waistcoat fastening a great iron bar across the door. They were in a small chamber, like a guard room, furnished with weapons and armour.

"Rahul!" gasped the Druid. "How did you…?"

The man turned and grinned. "You think we couldn't escape from those pathetic ropes, my friend? We are Thieves of Ur!"

A second man, thinner, with a droopy moustache, showed them a small sliver of knife blade that he had concealed in his sleeve. "We would never dream of going *anywhere* unprepared," he said, and gave a little bow. "We have been trying to find you."

"And now you have," said the Druid, holding his side and looking even paler. "In the nick of time. But I'm afraid we need to leave – urgently. Those dragons are after us, and so are a couple of rather nasty agents of the dark. Dora – is there any chance you could conjure a portal?"

As he said this, his legs appeared to crumple under him and he toppled sideways. At the same time there was a thundering crash at the door and the metal bar started to bend. Rahul and his friend snatched up two swords from the armoury and started towards the doorway.

"Go! Go!" shouted Rahul. "Ishmel and I can deal with these fellows!"

"Assuredly," said Ishmel, whirling his sword with an evil grin. "And when you're gone, we'll run. No one will care about two lowly thieves. And then we'll head back to headquarters – to deal with that traitor Nasir!"

Jem, who had managed to catch the Druid awkwardly as he fell, looked up at Dora, his face white.

"We've got to leave now! Can you do it? Can you get us back to the kingdom?"

Dora could hear more rumbling around them and taste dust in the air. Jem was right. They needed to get out. But where exactly? All they had with them were objects from Roland Castle – and that was the *last* place they wanted to arrive.

"I haven't got anything I can use," she cried. "I *knew* there was something important I forgot! I meant to bring something from my village – so we could go back there! In the rush I forgot. Oh, Jem! What an *idiot* I am!"

She slumped down next to the Druid. She felt like banging her head against the stone floor. How could she have forgotten to bring something they could use to return safely?

"Can we use something to go to Inanna's rooms?" said Jem. "At least we'll get away from the labyrinth!"

Dora shook her head. "You can only open a portal to another world," she said. "Not a different bit of the same world. It's too similar."

The Druid, who seemed to be on the edge of consciousness, plucked at her sleeve.

"Roland Castle?" he breathed.

"No good," said Jem. "That's what we came to tell you. Ravenglass has taken the castle."

The Druid closed his eyes for a moment, and then opened them. With a wince, he reached into his coat with his good arm and pulled out a small piece of yellow and orange card, slightly stained with blood.

"Use this," he whispered to Dora.

Dubiously, she held up the card. On it were printed the words: *Cheap Day Return, London to Basingstoke*. She could feel that the card came from Simon and Cat's world – but she wasn't at all sure that arriving in the middle of that non-magical world with the injured Druid and a princess of Ur-Akkad was the best of plans.

As she hesitated, there was a thud and a splitting sound, and a long crack appeared in the wooden door. They had seconds left before either Smith and Jones or the dragon came crashing into the chamber.

"Dora! *Now!*" said Jem. "Conjure the portal now!"

Dora held the card shakily in front of her and said the words of the portal spell. A swirling white mist materialised in front of them. Jem, Inanna and Dora, half dragging, half carrying the Druid, stumbled through the portal into the grey twilight of a London railway station platform.

PART SIX

PART SIX

Chapter Seventeen

Sir Bedwyr was feeling light-headed and blood kept dripping into his eyes from the gash on his forehead, but he needed to keep going. Dora had told him to find Albert Jemmet and he was determined not to let her down. It had been a close thing, escaping Lord Ravenglass's men, but he knew the castle better than they did, and after he'd disarmed three or four and knocked a couple more out cold, he'd managed to slip out of a small side gate. Unfortunately he hadn't had time to get properly dressed and he was feeling distinctly chilly as well as rather faint. But at least he was now on the forest road, and he had a horse – a rather sway-backed old nag he'd borrowed from a passing tinker.

He peered ahead, wondering if the stocky

fellow he could see plodding along the track just beyond the old mill was Albert Jemmet. He kicked the nag's sides, and as she ambled into a trot he winced and called out.

"Albert! I say, Albert!"

The man turned, startled.

"Sir Bedwyr! What in the name of the Great Tree…?"

"I've – I've been looking for you," said Sir Bedwyr faintly. The blood was roaring in his ears and the world around him started to fade alarmingly. "I – er – I don't feel exactly…" His voice trailed off, and the next thing he knew he appeared to be lying on the ground, staring up at a pair of anxious dark eyes that were peering at him out of a very long hairy face. Sir Bedwyr wondered where on earth he was and why no one had brought him any breakfast.

The long, hairy face snuffled gently at his ears, and Sir Bedwyr realised it was a horse. Then a hand started to lift him gently, and he heard Albert's voice.

"Pesky knight. What in the forest's name are you doing wandering around the countryside in this kind of state? And in your underwear, too?"

"Albert…" said Sir Bedwyr in a rather hoarse whisper. "I need to tell you something… It's important."

"It'll wait," said Albert firmly, giving him a friendly pat on the shoulder. "First we need to get you to an inn and sort out that head wound. And you look as if you could do with something to eat."

Sir Bedwyr allowed himself to drift off, feeling as if a great weight had been taken off his shoulders. Sausages, he thought happily. Grilled mushrooms. Nice hot scrambled eggs. And then he could tell Albert whatever it was he was supposed to pass on… Something about the Druid. Something about… What was it now? His head felt as if a hundred cows were trampling it into a field of shattered glass. The shards were splintering in front of his eyes, gleaming in the last rays of the setting sun, all orange and golden, the colour of… Amber! That was it! The amber.

Sir Bedwyr hauled himself up and clutched at Albert's shoulder.

"The amber," he choked. "The Druid went to get the amber… But Ravenglass's men have taken over the castle! They'll take it from him as soon as he returns!"

After bandaging his head and dealing with his other minor injuries, Albert Jemmet left Sir Bedwyr in the capable hands of the innkeeper's wife. He was to rest the night and then follow Albert to the forest in the morning. The innkeeper's wife was more than happy to tend to the needs of the handsome young knight, and was busy preparing a hearty stew and one of her famous apple pies as Albert set off.

Even with Sir Bedwyr's borrowed horse, it took Albert a few hours to reach the edge of the forest. He wasn't sure, in fact, whether he'd have been quicker walking. The horse was a stubborn old beast with a mind of its own, and Albert was not a good horseman. It was one of the many reasons he'd chosen to be an agent in a world where cars existed and horses were strictly for those who liked that sort of thing. However, after a detour for a leisurely drink at a brook not far from the cart track, the horse finally consented to amble into the forest with Albert still clutching on to its back.

He didn't stay on its back for long. Almost as soon as they entered, they got caught in a minor rift between worlds, and the horse was startled out of its few wits by the sight of a gleaming sky-capsule whizzing straight for it. By the time the capsule had winked out of existence, the horse was history and Albert was sitting on his bottom in a very damp patch of nettles.

He glanced around for his pack, which was lying in a nest of brambles not far away. As he hauled himself to his feet, something that looked like a small blue bird fluttered through the nearby trees and landed on a branch next to his head.

"Thank goodness!" said the bird, who now looked rather more like a large blue caterpillar. "We need your help!"

"Caractacus," said Albert, nodding in greeting. "Good to see you."

"Albert," replied the caterpillar. "Good to see you too and so on and so forth. But really – we have a bit of a crisis on our hands. No time for small talk."

Albert brushed himself down and patted his pockets as if to check everything was in one piece.

Then he nodded briskly. "Yes. Well, you tell me your crisis and I'll tell you mine."

Caractacus frowned. "*Another* problem?"

Albert looked grim. "Ravenglass has attacked and taken Roland Castle. So when – if – the Druid returns with the amber, Ravenglass's men will have it. What's worse, young Dora and Jem have apparently gone to the Akkadian Empire to warn him, so now we've got those two to worry about rescuing as well. And there's a fool of a knight on his way to you when he's recovered from his injuries – name of Sir Bedwyr."

"Ah," said Caractacus. "Good news on all fronts, then."

"And your crisis?" said Albert.

"Simon and Cat," said Caractacus. "We had them here in the forest – but they've gone. The guardians did their best to stop them but it seems Cat used the amber. The trees report that she used it to go to the palace."

There was a silence as Albert digested this news. He rubbed his chin thoughtfully.

"There's something wrong here," he said. "Why would they go to the palace? They know enough about Ravenglass to steer clear of him…"

Caractacus nodded. "We are concerned that Lukos may have got involved directly."

Albert looked up, startled. "Lukos? But could he? Does he have the power?"

"He can't use magic, of course. But there are other ways. We wondered if… their father? Gwyn?"

Albert's eyes widened and he swore colourfully and solidly for a good two minutes. Caractacus waited patiently for him to run out of further expletives.

"Indeed," was all he said when Albert had finished.

"Right," said Albert, gathering his breath. "I'll be after them, then."

"If you would, Albert. They know you and trust you," the blue caterpillar said. "Meanwhile I'll see what I can find out about what's going on in the Akkadian Empire… If you manage to find them and bring them to their senses, you'll need to get them out of the palace with all speed. And watch out – if Ravenglass has the amber already, you could be in trouble."

Albert nodded. "Don't worry, I'll be careful. And if I find them, I'll take them home. The house is warded, and besides – their mother's there. I have a feeling they might need to see her once I've got them away from the palace."

He picked up his pack and slung it on his shoulders, and then, with a cheery wave at Caractacus, he set off purposefully into the forest.

Chapter Eighteen

Cat was finding it hard to get to sleep. She and Simon had been given separate rooms in the north tower of the palace, and a magnificent supper had been laid out for them in the adjoining sitting room. Lord Ravenglass had ordered a steaming hot bath and fresh clothes for them both, and assigned them each a servant to look after them. *Or watch over us*, thought Cat, and then was surprised at the thought, which seemed to have come unbidden into her mind.

She was lying in a cosy four-poster bed, with rich velvet curtains drawn back to let in the pale moonlight from her turret window. She felt clean and warm and safe – yet she couldn't settle down. Something was bothering her, but she couldn't put her finger on what it was. She glanced over to where her servant – May? Myrtle? – was dozing in a large armchair. Just beyond her was the door to the sitting room, and beyond that was Simon's bedroom, with another ornately carved four-poster. He'd bounced up and down on it happily and then wrapped himself in the velvet covers, his sword placed carefully with his clothes at the foot of the bed, and waved her a sleepy goodnight. His servant, Ollie, had settled down by the sitting-room fire, polishing Simon's new boots, but he'd no doubt be snoring now, same as Myrtle.

Cat lay awake, watching the moonlight slowly move across the wall, wondering what it was that felt wrong. Absentmindedly she put her hand up to her throat to feel for the amber – and then she remembered that it wasn't there. She'd given it to Lord Ravenglass. But her fingers caught hold of something else, another pendant. It was her silver locket, she realised, and with that thought came another. There was something important about the locket, something she needed to remember, but she couldn't – it was as if there was a fog in her brain. Cat lay still, holding the locket and straining after a thought that seemed just out of reach… But as she almost caught at the edge of it, there was a crash from the sitting room and she sat bolt upright in shock.

"W-what? Who's there?" she called. Myrtle had barely stirred, but a figure in the sitting room approached her door and peered in, bowing apologetically.

"A hundred pardons, my lady!" Ollie called in a low voice. "It was me. I fell asleep and slipped off the footstool. Knocked the table over. Please... go back to sleep!"

Cat pushed back the covers and padded out to the door. She was wearing what passed for nightwear in the kingdom but felt more like proper clothes to her – a heavy cotton tunic and warm velvet leggings. She gave him a friendly grin.

"It doesn't matter," she said. "I couldn't sleep anyway. I'll come and join you by the fire – we can finish off the last bits of supper."

Ollie blushed and looked at his toes. He was a tall, lanky lad, a year or so older than her, Cat thought. But he was obviously not used to consorting with fine ladies in their nightwear. Cat gave him an encouraging pat on the back, which made him blush even harder, and indicated the chairs by the fireplace.

"Come on," she said. "You can tell me all about the palace. I know nothing. But… I'm worried. Something's not right. Maybe you can help me work out what."

Ollie swallowed, and nodded, and they settled down by the fire with a plate of leftovers between them. Cat was good at drawing people out, and before long Ollie was telling her all about his home village and his job at the palace – the strict hierarchies and rules, and the problem of staying on the right side of Lord Ravenglass.

"So," said Cat cheerfully, demolishing the last of a bowl of sticky dates. "Have you ever done anything really bad? Anything you'd get really punished for if they found out?"

Ollie hesitated, as if trying to decide something. "Do you promise not to tell anyone?"

Cat nodded.

"Well, then," said Ollie. "There was this thing – only a week or so ago. I got lost in the cellars and I found a man in some sort of strange ice cave, chained up. It was… like a place that wasn't really there, if you know what I mean. And then Lord Ravenglass came down to talk to him, and I scarpered." He looked across at Cat, frowning.

"Thing is – I think they mentioned your name. When they were talking… Catrin, they said. And Simon. That's you and your brother, isn't it?"

Cat nodded, her eyes fixed on Ollie's dark brown ones. "What – what did you think of him? The man in chains?" she said, and held her breath. It felt as if his answer was somehow very important.

Ollie held her gaze. "He frightened me," he said. "He was the scariest person I've ever seen. Including Lord Ravenglass."

Cat let out her breath in a rush. That was it! That was what was bothering her! Despite the fact that the man in the ice appeared to be her dad, despite the fact that she was convinced with her rational mind that he was, in fact, Gwyn Arnold, there was something about him that made her feel very, very frightened.

Cat leant over to Ollie and said in a low tone, "There's something wrong here. I'm not sure what. But I need to find out. Will you help me?"

Ollie straightened his shoulders and nodded. "Of course. If I can."

"Good," said Cat. "I wonder… could you take me to the queen?"

Ollie turned pale.

"Th—the queen?" he said. "Me – an ordinary under-footman? If I'm found anywhere near the queen's chambers they'll sack me on the spot!"

"Please," said Cat. "I think she might be the only one who knows what's going on. It's *really* important!"

Ollie swallowed, and then nodded. "Okay. I might be able to get you there. I know a few shortcuts. With a bit of luck we won't be seen."

"Excellent!" said Cat, and gave him a beaming smile. Ollie blushed again, and they tiptoed together to the door.

Although it was well past midnight, the corridors of the palace were by no means empty. A few servants were still in evidence, hauling wood for fires, collecting boots to clean, taking late-night snacks to wakeful lords or courtiers. And some of those courtiers themselves were reeling back to their quarters after a late-night drinking party, or scurrying about dealing with some impossible task set by Lord Ravenglass or one of his deputies. Cat and Ollie had to move cautiously, and frequently found themselves diving into an alcove or behind a tapestry to let a group of noisy third-degree noblemen march past.

They were just about to emerge from one of these alcoves, not far from the queen's rooms, when Cat saw something that made her feel suddenly cold. Stalking along the corridor were two tall, thin figures with black hair, dressed in identical glossy black suits. They were walking purposefully towards Lord Ravenglass's chambers, and the air around them almost crackled with the force of their anger.

Cat froze. As the two men passed the alcove, she turned to Ollie. "Can we follow them?" she mouthed. He hesitated, and then beckoned her back the way they'd come. Hardly making a sound, he led her into a large unlit chamber. In one wall, two ornate double doors obviously led into the adjoining room, but they were closed, the glowing light from the room beyond just visible through the crack where the doors met.

Tiptoeing to the doors, they found they could hear voices from the other side, and when Cat put her eye to the crack, she glimpsed one of the dark-suited figures as he stalked past, and heard his nasal voice.

"Gone! When we broke into the chamber there were just two local idiots, who scarpered. The forest agents must have taken the fire amber to another world, but there's no trace of where."

"We'll find them," said a second voice. "And when we do… we'll *crush* them."

The second voice was dry, hoarse. Cat had heard it before. It made her feel light-headed with fear.

"Your zeal does not in the least make up for your *incompetence*," came a third voice. It was Lord Ravenglass, and he sounded to be in a fine temper. "This is the second time you've failed. Worlds above! Must I do everything myself? It's just as well for you that the other part of our plans is proceeding satisfactorily. We have the earth amber from the girl. It's a start. We'll just have to work on recovering the fire amber another way."

There was a murmur – from Mr Smith, Cat thought – and then the voice of Lord Ravenglass again, icy with anger.

"Oh go away, both of you! Come back when you have something more positive to report. But if you fail me again… *I'll have your eyes*."

Cat found she was trembling. She couldn't

think straight. One part of her seemed to be rejoicing in the news that Lord Ravenglass had failed to get the fire amber – another part of her was devastated. How would they save her father without it? Gradually she became aware of Ollie, standing next to her. His hand was on her shoulder and his worried face close to hers.

"Are you all right, Lady Catrin?" he was whispering. "Are you ill?"

Cat shook her head. "No – no, I'm fine. Can – can we go and find the queen, now?"

Ollie nodded and took her by the hand. She felt peculiar – as if she were not really in her body. Her head was pounding but she could barely feel any other part of her. Ollie pulled her along gently and she followed, trying to focus but not really succeeding.

Luckily they met no one else. The queen's quarters were very close by and there was no guard on the plain, narrow servant's corridor that ran parallel to the official entrance. The queen's lady-in-waiting was fast asleep in the antechamber by the fire, and the queen herself was snoring like a rhinoceros in the middle of her ornate four-poster bed. Cat closed the bedroom door gently and then turned to the rather plump figure in the bed.

"This is the queen?' she said to Ollie, surprised by how un-regal the old lady looked. Ollie, rather pale, nodded.

"If I'm found here, in her bedroom, they'll – they'll probably hang me," he said in a faint voice, as if suddenly rather appalled at what Cat had managed to persuade him to do.

"It'll be all right," whispered Cat, although she wasn't convinced it would be. For some reason it had seemed important to go to the queen, but now she was here she wasn't sure what to do. Her hand went up to her throat and she pulled absently at the locket. As she did so, she noticed that around the queen's neck was what was obviously the kingdom's own piece of amber, a glowing jewel on a silver chain. Cat reached out to touch it with her other hand, and as she did so the queen opened her eyes.

Cat jumped backwards, startled, as the queen sat up. Ollie dived instantly under the bed and pulled his long legs in after him. The queen pushed her white hair back from her face and turned her blue eyes questioningly on Cat.

"Umm... Y-your M-majesty..." stammered Cat. Her head was really pounding now, but in the middle of the beat that was reverberating round her skull there was a small voice that appeared to be urging: *Open the locket... open the locket... open the locket.*

The queen smiled at her and reached out to point at the pendant round Cat's neck.

"There's a really *fizzing* halo of magic round that pendant," she said in an interested voice. "Has it got a ghost in it?"

Great-Aunt Irene! thought Cat. Of course! How could she have forgotten? Great-Aunt Irene had folded herself into the locket and said that if they ever needed her, they just had to open it. Cat clutched at the pendant, and at the same time the voice in her head seemed to grow to the volume of a shout. *JUST OPEN THE LOCKET!*

Blindly Cat felt for the clasp and got her fingernails under it. She pulled apart the two halves of the locket and out of it flew a quantity of silvery dust, which almost immediately resolved itself into the shape of a rather stately old lady with a silvery cane.

"At last!" she said, rapping her cane on the

floor with a very real-sounding tap. "Couldn't think how to get past that spell Ravenglass put you under. But getting you to the queen seemed like it might help. And now I'm finally out, we can take that enchantment off you and start making plans."

She beamed at Cat and then bowed to Queen Igraine, who was looking rather startled. Then she frowned down at the floor and pointed with her cane at Ollie's boots, sticking out from under the bed.

"Would somebody care to tell me," she said in a disapproving voice, "who is on the other end of those feet?"

Chapter Nineteen

For a rather portly man, Albert Jemmet was surprisingly light on his feet. He had managed to climb almost to the ramparts of the palace using a convenient tree and an ancient rusting pipe designed to carry water from the palace roof to the kitchen garden below. Now he was resting, in the corner between a buttress and the East Tower, and contemplating the final bit of the climb.

He'd arrived at the palace just before dawn, but the sky was starting to lighten now and pink streaks were visible in the east. Albert took a deep breath and reached up, finding a slight crack between the stones for his fingers to get a purchase. He felt with his boots for a tiny ledge a few feet above where he was standing, uttered a quick prayer to the guardians of the forest, and started to climb.

Five minutes later, after a couple of heart-stopping moments when he'd missed his foothold, Albert hauled himself astride the ramparts and looked to left and right. He'd deliberately chosen the oldest and least-used corner of the palace, and his luck held. There were no guards patrolling. Albert slipped over the wall and moved swiftly towards a small door that led into the East Tower.

Simon woke to find Albert Jemmet sitting on the end of his bed, chewing a toothpick.

"Aha," Albert said, when he saw Simon looking at him. He pointed with the toothpick. "You've led us a merry dance and no mistake."

Simon's head hurt. He felt strangely pleased to see Albert's shrewd, no-nonsense face beaming at him, and then immediately appalled. Albert was a forest agent. He'd helped to capture and imprison his dad! Simon reached for his sword, but Albert put his hand down on it firmly.

"Not a good idea," he said. "I'm not sure what sort of nonsense Ravenglass has been telling you, and I'm not about to let you use that sword on me before we sort out what's what. Where's Cat?"

Simon glanced through the bedroom door at

the empty sitting room. "I don't know – isn't she in her bed?"

Albert shook his head. "Servant's asleep – I put a hex on her myself to keep her that way – but Cat appears to have gone."

Simon ran his hands through his hair. He wasn't sure whether he should shout for help or try to run for it. More than anything, he found that Albert's presence on the bed was making him feel very relieved, but he couldn't work out at all why that should be.

Albert leant forward and gently took hold of Simon's shoulders. He looked seriously into his eyes and then sighed.

"So... was it your dad?"

"My... dad?" said Simon, feeling light-headed and peculiar.

"Did he appear as your dad?"

Simon felt as if he had swallowed a piece of lead. He could feel the weight of it travelling down his throat and settling heavily in his stomach. He opened his mouth, and then closed it again. He nodded.

Albert's blue eyes were as angry as Simon had ever seen them. He passed his hands over

Simon's head, as if wiping away cobwebs, and then brushed them together briskly.

"Had a spell on you," he said shortly. "You'd nearly broken it yourself. He'd have had to renew it today for sure." He patted Simon on the knee and then handed him the sword.

"This was your dad's sword," he said. "You can wear it proudly. He was a good man, and a great friend to the forest. But he is dead, Simon. I'm sorry."

Simon closed his eyes. He felt as if a yawning hole had just opened up beneath him, as if he was plummeting down to the depths of the earth. His hand closed on the sword hilt and he gripped it hard, and then opened his eyes.

"If that wasn't Dad, then… who?" he said. His voice was croaky.

"Lukos," said Albert. "He's a shape-shifter. He can appear as anyone. He knew what your dad looked like – they'd crossed swords before, so to speak."

"When?" said Simon.

"Long time ago now. They were forest agents, your dad and Lou. Did you know that?' said Albert. "Good ones, too. It was a thumping loss to the forest when your dad died, and Lou decided to retire. They did good service last time Lukos started causing trouble."

"Did they – had they been there? To the ice cave?" said Simon, shivering.

"No – no one can get there without all four bits of amber. But they'd seen him, talked with him. Fought with his servants. The place where he's imprisoned – it shifts. When it connects to a world… Well, sometimes he manages to make contact with people there, persuade them to work for the dark. Your dad helped stop a terrible war Lukos was waging – oh, must have been twenty years ago now."

He put his hand out, rubbing his thumb down the engravings on the sword between them. "I helped in that one," he said. "Me, your dad, the Druid. We stopped his little game. But Lukos is always a threat, even imprisoned."

"And he – put a spell on me?" said Simon.

Albert shook his head. "Not Lukos – he can't do magic across the barrier. Ravenglass will have put it on you when you got here."

"But that means before – in the forest…"

"Yes," said Albert gently. "It means Lukos

managed to trick you at first without any enchantment." He put his hand out and squeezed Simon's shoulder. "It's nothing to be ashamed of. He's very powerful and very clever. He's a master at holding out to people what they want most in the world."

Simon swallowed, and brushed the back of his hand across his eyes. He took the hilt of the sword, letting his other hand run down the length of the beautiful engraved blade. So it was true – his dad was really dead, and this was all he had left of him.

"You have us," said Albert, as if reading his mind. "You have all his friends – the forest folk, the Druid, me. And your mum. I was wondering – maybe we should get you back to her, eh? What do you say?"

Simon looked up, and nodded. But then he frowned and sat up straighter. "Albert!" he said urgently. "The amber! Cat gave Ravenglass her amber. We'll have to get it back!"

But at that precise moment, the door to the sitting room banged open and Cat tumbled in, followed by Ollie and a rather silvery old lady with a cane.

"Albert!" Cat said as she saw him. "How did *you* get here?" Then she turned to Simon and saw his expression. She walked over to the bed and held out her arms, and they hugged each other tightly.

After a few minutes, Albert put his hand on her shoulder and patted it sympathetically, and she looked up, her face tear-stained but determined.

"I've released Great-Aunt Irene," she said, gesturing at the silvery old lady. "And we've talked to the queen. We've come up with a plan for getting back the amber!"

Chapter Twenty

Simon was sweating, and Lord Ravenglass was in his shirtsleeves. Behind his transparent barrier, the gaunt man with silver chains was urging them both on and clapping.

"Parry!" gasped Lord Ravenglass. "Parry... and left... and right... and now! Under the guard – good!"

He put up his sword and Simon did the same, both of them breathing heavily.

"Well done!" said Lord Ravenglass when he had got his breath back. "Astonishing progress for only one morning, Simon. You're a natural!"

Simon nodded, shortly. He was doing his best to appear pleased, and eager, and in all respects still convinced that the man in the ice cave was his father, but he was having to grit his teeth not

213

to let his anger show. In some ways it helped that they were fighting – Simon's resentment and fury at being tricked could be safely expressed through his savage assaults on Lord Ravenglass in the name of practice.

"Could we try that one again?" he said. "I'm not sure I got it." He twirled the sword and jabbed, practising the manoeuvre. His muscles were aching and he could barely see straight, but he knew he had to keep Ravenglass occupied down here for as long as possible.

"What do you think, Gwyn?" called Lord Ravenglass to the man in the ice, who was standing by the barrier and watching Simon intently. "Enthusiastic, your boy, eh?"

"Very… enthusiastic," said the man, his blue eyes thoughtful. He beckoned Simon towards him. "You've got a gift. It's in the blood, you know. You're descended from the man that sword was forged for… Bruni the one-eyed." As he said the name, his mouth twisted strangely, as if it pained him.

"So you must be descended from him as well," said Simon, his voice neutral. "Aren't you?"

The man looked hard at Simon, and frowned. After a heartbeat, he said, "Yes. Do you doubt it?"

Simon looked down. *Too pointed*, he thought. He mustn't let them suspect that he knew.

"I just wondered," he said nervously. "Maybe it was from Mum's side rather than yours… But that's mad, of course. It was your sword, after all, wasn't it? So you must be Bruni's heir, too."

The man watched him for a moment.

"Yes – it was my sword," he said finally, and then smiled warmly. "And you're learning to use it in fine style. Ravenglass?" As Simon moved away, Lukos gestured to Lord Ravenglass to approach. Simon watched as the two consulted in low voices. He wiped the sweat from his face with the velvet jacket that he'd thrown aside as he started fighting.

After a while, Lord Ravenglass came over and ruffled Simon's hair in a friendly gesture.

"Well done, my boy," he said. "A good day's progress. But I think maybe you'd better get back to your sister now. She'll be bored, stuck in your chambers with just Myrtle for company."

Simon nodded, and Lord Ravenglass pulled on his embroidered velvet coat and sheathed his sword. As they left, Simon saw him turn to the prisoner and make an odd gesture. The man, his blue eyes burning into Simon's brown ones, nodded slowly and then raised his hand to Simon in farewell.

Simon gave him a thumb's up sign and tried to grin, but his mouth didn't feel as if it was wholly cooperating. He had a feeling it had come out rather more like a grimace. Lord Ravenglass patted him on the back and ushered him out of the cellar and up the spiral staircase. Simon crossed his fingers and hoped Cat and the others had had enough time to do what they needed to do.

Lord Ravenglass's chambers were usually cleaned every morning by the senior under-footman and the chief chambermaid. Today, however, the senior under-footman had been struck down by a terrible stomach ache, and Ollie Bowbuckle had heroically offered to take his place. Very few of the servants liked going anywhere near Lord Ravenglass's rooms, so they were thoroughly grateful for Ollie's self-sacrifice. The chief chambermaid, Verity Pond, was particularly pleased, as she had had a bit of a crush on Ollie ever since the young lad had been taken on at the palace.

As they opened the door to Lord Ravenglass's

antechamber, Verity turned to Ollie with a smile she'd been practising for ages in the mirror and said brightly, "So, would you like to do the privy, or shall I?"

To her amazement, Ollie grabbed her round the waist and gave her a passionate kiss on the lips while kicking the door shut behind them with one foot. Verity barely had time to return the embrace before she felt the light touch of a spell, and the next moment she was out cold on the floor.

Albert Jemmet, standing just behind her, wagged his finger at Ollie and shook his head in mock disapproval. "I said distract her, young man. Kissing was not called for."

Ollie looked sheepish. "I've been meaning to do that for ages," he said. "It seemed the ideal opportunity. And you have to admit, it *did* distract her."

Cat, emerging from behind a tapestry, grinned at him. "You might have some explaining to do when we revive her," she said. "But really, it's worked out quite well. You can tell her she fainted from the shock!"

Ollie blushed, and grinned back. "I think she liked it," he said.

Great-Aunt Irene rapped her cane on the floor in an imperious manner. "Enough foolishness," she said. "We have to get this amber while Simon's distracting Ravenglass. To work!"

It didn't take them very long to find the place where Lord Ravenglass had put the amber. It was in full view, in a glass display case very close to his bed. The tricky part was going to be undoing all the hexes and spells that surrounded it without setting off any magical alarms or booby traps. Great-Aunt Irene contemplated the amber for a few minutes then turned to Cat.

"I can see the spells," she said. "It's one of the advantages of being dead. One can see in so many more dimensions. But I can't do any magic myself, so I rather think you're going to have to do it, my dear."

Cat was taken aback. "But Albert..." she said.

"Not up to this sort of thing," said Albert cheerfully. "This is deep magic – Ravenglass is a master. But you've got the ability, Cat. It's in the blood. And your great-aunt will help."

"W-what do I have to do?" said Cat.

Great-Aunt Irene gave her an encouraging smile. "There's no time to teach you the niceties,

I'm afraid," she said. "I think the best thing is if I hold on to you. Then you should be able to see the spells the way I see them. After that it's... Well – you just need to unravel them."

Cat felt Great-Aunt Irene's ghostly hands take hold of her, like two delicate icy bits of lace settling onto her shoulders, and suddenly she could see that the glass cabinet in front of her was covered in silvery strands of spell-work. She approached it cautiously and put her hand out to the nearest strand. She could see where it looped across the cabinet door, and the way it was entwined with another silvery strand that passed the door in the other direction.

"Just gently pull them apart," came Great-Aunt Irene's voice from over her shoulder. "But at the same time, use your magic to dissolve them. Think of them as made of ice. Use the warmth of your hands to melt them."

Cat took hold of one of the strands and tried to imagine it as a filigree of ice... As she pulled at it carefully and steadily, she saw that it was indeed fading, shimmering into nothing. More confidently, she took hold of the next piece and willed it to disappear, melt away. With growing excitement she realised that the many silvery spells that surrounded the cabinet were all fading, one after the other, as her counter-magic passed down the threads. Finally, the door clicked open, and she reached in cautiously. There was one final spell on the amber – darker and thicker than the others. Cat took hold of it and shivered. It was almost as if Lord Ravenglass were standing there, his elegant white hands holding hers in a cold grip. Her whole body felt frozen, and the cold seemed to be seeping along her veins, reaching into her mind.

"Don't let the spell get you!" said Great-Aunt Irene urgently in her ear. "Fight it, Cat! Break it – now!"

Cat made a huge effort to move, and found she could just twitch her fingers. Quickly, before the spell froze her again, she pulled at the strand and sent a fierce command down to her fingertips: Dissolve! For a moment it was like pushing against a barrier and then, with a sudden lurch, the spell was gone, and the amber was in her hands.

Cat gave a great sigh of relief and slipped the chain over her head. As she looked around, she saw that Albert and Ollie between them had cleaned and tidied the room, and bright sunshine was flooding in from the arched window by Lord Ravenglass's bed.

"H-how long?' she asked, confused.

"Three hours," said Albert. "Tricky spells though – well done, Cat! But now I think we need to scarper, pronto. Young Simon won't be able to keep them busy much longer."

He turned to Great-Aunt Irene. "You'll be coming with us," he said. "But what do we do about the queen?"

Great-Aunt Irene looked troubled. "I think we'll have to leave her here," she said. "I couldn't persuade her otherwise. She says her place is in the kingdom. She insists she's on her guard now, and more than a match for Ravenglass." She sniffed. "Of course, she would be if she had all her wits. As it is, he certainly won't get the amber off her… Unless he can draw on the power of the other pieces."

"Then we'll just have to make sure he doesn't get them," said Albert grimly. "Meanwhile, young Ollie will be here." He put his hand on Ollie's shoulder and looked at him with a serious expression. "You'll have to be our agent here, for now. Can you keep an eye on the queen? Stand ready if we need you?"

Ollie nodded solemnly, and then bowed to Cat. "Good luck, Lady Catrin," he said. "I hope we meet again."

She grinned and gave him a thump on the back. Then she, Great-Aunt Irene and Albert slipped out of the door. Just as they left, Albert snapped his fingers over Verity's prostrate form and she opened her eyes.

"W-what?" she said, looking round in confusion.

"You fainted," said Ollie, and winked at her. "So I did all the cleaning by myself."

Simon got back to their North Tower chambers to find that Cat, Albert and Great-Aunt Irene were all there and had already conjured a portal. The shimmering misty doorway stood in the corner of Cat's bedroom, and Albert was holding the slightly battered old screwdriver he'd used to conjure it.

"It'll take us back to my workshop," he said as he saw Simon looking at the screwdriver. "Thought it safest, all in all. Don't want to go materialising in the kitchen of your house right in front of your mum, do we?"

"Was it all right?" said Cat, giving Simon a squeeze on the shoulder. Her blue eyes, so like Gwyn's, were sympathetic.

Simon nodded. "It was – a bit difficult. But mostly I was too busy learning to use a sword. There wasn't too much talking. Did you get the amber?"

Cat pulled the jewel out from under her T-shirt and showed him. Her expression was triumphant. "I did magic to get it," she said. "Me! It was amazing!"

"Well done," said Simon, but he felt rather put out at the news. Cat had the amber, after all. It wasn't fair if she got to be a spell-user as well.

"Enough chit-chat," said Great-Aunt Irene. "We need to go. Albert – your arm…"

Albert took Great-Aunt Irene's arm and strode into the misty doorway. Simon looked at Cat and they both stepped smartly after him. Behind them, the mist popped out of existence.

Albert's workshop was a large lock-up garage on the edge of Wemworthy. It was full of strange contraptions and old bits of broken motorbike. In pride of place at one end was a large old-fashioned armchair, and next to that was a small table with a paraffin stove, a kettle, mugs and a teapot. Albert hesitated a moment in front of the stove and then shrugged.

"We can get a cup of tea at your mum's," he said. "Best be getting on."

"How are we going to get there?" said Cat.

Albert grinned and strode to the front of the lock-up, where a heavy old tarpaulin was tucked lovingly around an oddly-shaped object. Pulling the tarpaulin back, he pointed to an extremely battered old motorbike and adjacent sidecar.

"My trusty Norton," he said proudly. "You can ride pillion, Cat. Simon and your great-aunt can share the sidecar."

PART SEVEN

Chapter Twenty-one

The fact that it was dusk, and rush hour, meant that the sudden appearance of four strange figures on Platform 6 of London's Waterloo Station passed unnoticed. But even in rush hour, it proved impossible for Dora, Jem and Inanna to manoeuvre the heavily bleeding Druid along the platform without attracting attention.

"Oh my God, he's been shot!" cried a woman in very high heels, her hand to her mouth.

"What's going on here?"

"Call the police!"

"Easy there, easy now," said a sturdy young man with dreadlocks, who had moved forward to catch the Druid as he slumped to the ground. "What happened? Are you all right?" He felt the damp patch on the Druid's jacket and then looked at the blood on his hand in shock. "He's been stabbed. Someone call an ambulance!"

The woman in high heels fumbled for her phone and a crowd started to gather. Dora, Jem and Inanna moved protectively round the Druid, not quite sure what to do. The man who'd caught the Druid put his hand out to Inanna, who was trembling, and asked if she was all right.

"Were you with him? Did you see who did it?"

Inanna shook her head. "I–I–I don't… I can't," she said, and her hand went to her mouth. "Everything feels wrong!" she wailed.

Jem put his arm round her and made soothing noises. Dora could see that she was suffering from the shock of being in a new world – one that was utterly different to her own. Dora herself was finding the station an extremely alien place and even though she'd been prepared for the flat, unmagical feel of Simon and Cat's world, the noise of the trains and the crackling announcements and the press of people was making her head ache.

An older woman pushed her way through the crowd and knelt down by the Druid.

"I'm a nurse," she said. "Let me have a look

at him." The young man moved away to give her room and she gently started to examine the Druid's wounds.

"It's all right, it's under control," the young man said. He gestured at the crowds. "Give the guy some space, now. Move along."

Gradually the press of people lessened and the man turned to Dora.

"Is he your dad?" he said, indicating the Druid, who was now completely unconscious. "Is there anyone I can call? Your mum, maybe?"

Dora gave him a bewildered look. Call? How was he going to call anyone useful to this obscure corner of a non-magical world? He couldn't possibly know any summoning spells!

"On the *mobile*," said Jem, who had paid more attention to the electronic innovations of this world last time he'd been here. "He means on a mobile phone. Like Cat's."

He turned to the man confidently. "No – there's no one. Just us, and our... er... dad. Will he be all right?"

The woman looked up and nodded. "He's lost a lot of blood," she said. "But he should be fine – if we can get him to a hospital."

As she spoke there was a commotion at the other end of the platform, and then two men in green overalls were heading towards them with a stretcher and a large bag of equipment. In no time, the Druid was trussed up on the stretcher and Dora, Jem and Inanna were being bundled along the platform and out into the busy main road. There, a bright yellow ambulance was waiting to rush them all to the accident and emergency department of St Thomas's Hospital.

The Druid had a broken wrist, a nasty stab wound to the chest, and a number of other cuts and bruises that appeared to have been administered with sharp blades. The police were less than happy with the inability of Jem, Dora or Inanna to account for the wounds or to give them any sensible explanation of who they were, where they lived, and why they were all in fancy dress. Eventually the sergeant in charge decided to allow them to remain with their 'father' for the night – mainly due to Dora's convincing tears and Inanna's tendency to bite anyone who tried to remove her. He told the hospital he would be making arrangements for them to go to temporary foster care in the morning, but until then, they could stay. The hospital staff managed to find some proper clothes for them all and generously moved some armchairs into the Druid's room for them to sleep on.

The Druid had been given painkillers and a strong sedative, so it was nearly dawn before he regained consciousness. Dora was hovering anxiously over his bed, wondering whether to shake him, when he twitched and opened his eyes. He took a moment to focus, and then grimaced.

"Where?" he said, his voice rather hoarse.

"Simon and Cat's world," she replied. "They took us to some sort of... healing place. A hospital, they said."

The Druid took a moment to digest this, and then looked down at his body, pinned to the bed with crisp cotton sheets and a blue blanket. His left arm was in a sling and he appeared to be wearing a blue hospital gown, tied at the back. He groaned.

"Awake then?" said Jem, jumping up from the chair where he'd been dozing. "At last! We need to get out of here, before they lock us all up in these foster places they've been threatening us with."

The Druid tried to sit up, but the blankets defeated him. Jem pulled them loose and gave him a hand to get upright. The Druid ran his uninjured hand through the bits of his hair that were not under a bandage, and then pinched the bridge of his nose, trying to focus. Inanna, who had been asleep on the floor by his bed, sat up and yawned.

"I am *not* impressed with this world at all!" she said. "The floor is extremely hard and the food is *disgusting*!"

The Druid glanced across at her and his shoulders slumped. "We have the princess of Ur-Akkad with us?" he said in disbelief. "Just to make things a *little* more difficult?"

Dora nodded apologetically. "She wanted to escape from Akkad – she's got magic, she was worried she'd be found out and imprisoned. And then at the end, it was all so fast. Smith and Jones were there. We couldn't just leave her behind…"

The Druid held up his hand to stop her. "It's all right. It's fine. I understand." He closed his eyes and thought for a few moments. When he opened them, he looked more cheerful.

"We'll go to Cat and Simon's house," he said. "If we get there early enough, Florence will be at work and we can get hold of them without her knowing. Then Cat can use her amber to send us to the forest."

"We've got the fire amber," said Jem, nodding at Inanna. "Could you use that one?"

The Druid gave Inanna an interested look. "You're wearing it?" he asked, and she nodded, her hand coming up to where the jewel was nestled just under her newly acquired T-shirt.

"It cooled down quite quickly after I picked it up," she said. "So I thought it was safest round my neck."

"It's very likely you're an heir," said the Druid thoughtfully. "You're of royal blood, after all. And it's quite possible you *could* use it. But it would be risky. Controlling a piece of amber when you've only just taken possession of it – all sorts of things could go wrong."

Dora frowned. "Cat did it fine."

"Cat," said the Druid with a smile, "is a very exceptional young lady. I wouldn't want to bet on it working out a second time. Besides, the fire amber is notoriously tricky."

Inanna raised one eyebrow. "I am sure I could use it if you showed me how," she said, tossing her head. The jewels in her braids clinked together as she gave the Druid a haughty look.

The Druid returned the look with a stern one of his own, and she dropped her gaze.

"Well," she said sulkily. "Whatever you think best."

"We'll go to Florence's," said the Druid firmly. "Inanna's too inexperienced. And right now I'm in no state to use the amber myself."

The Druid eased himself to the side of the bed and slipped his long legs out from under the covers. He grimaced.

"My clothes, Jem, if you'd be so kind," he said, his voice a little strained. Jem grabbed the Druid's clothes and started to help him into them. The sling made it extremely awkward, and by the time Jem had laced his boots and Dora had finished fastening his jacket, the Druid's breathing was rather ragged and his face was the colour of putty.

He pushed himself up and stood for a few moments.

"Er… I think we may have a problem," he said

faintly, and then sank back onto the bed. "I don't think I'll be able to walk."

Dora bit her lip, but Jem's face brightened. "I've got an idea!" he said, and disappeared out of the door. When he returned, he was pushing a large chair with wheels attached.

"I saw them when we arrived," he said cheerfully. "They're like small carts for people. You just push them around while someone sits in them. They're brilliant!"

The Druid gave Jem an approving look.

"Excellent," he said. "Should just about do it."

Escaping from St Thomas's Hospital took longer than they'd thought possible. They got hopelessly lost almost at once. All the corridors looked the same – in fact Dora was convinced it was the same corridor, multiplying as they walked down it like some strange replicating monster. Luckily, the bustling nurses and porters more or less ignored them – in a busy hospital, three children and a man in a wheelchair with a bandage round his head were not a remarkable sight. But as they hesitated yet again at a large junction of several corridors, a bald man carrying a bunch of flowers took pity on them and stopped to ask where they were going.

"We're trying to get out," said Jem, with a hint of desperation in his voice. "But we keep going round in circles."

The bald man laughed. "Terrible, isn't it?" he said cheerfully. "Here, I tell you what – I'm on my way to see my wife, but I can take you to the lifts. That'll get you down to the ground floor, then the exit's just a hop and a skip."

Jem raised his eyebrows at Dora and she shrugged. She had no idea what the man had just said, but at least they wouldn't be trudging down the same endless corridor all over again. They followed him to a set of double doors, where he pushed a small button. The doors swished open and he gestured at the large metallic box behind them.

"There you go," he said. "Ground floor."

It didn't look like any kind of floor to Dora, more like a prison cell. She wasn't at all happy about getting inside it. But Jem was pushing the Druid in and Inanna was following. As she stepped across the edge of the box after them, a man in a white coat came rushing in and pressed another button and the doors closed.

"Where do you want?" he said to them, his finger hesitating over the set of buttons. Almost immediately the box juddered.

"The ground," said Jem, just as Inanna gasped, "It's an earthquake!"

The man gave her a funny look and pressed a green button, and the juddering got worse. Now it felt as if the whole building was collapsing. Was Inanna right? Was it an earthquake?

The man seemed unconcerned, but Inanna was clutching at Jem.

"It's falling down!" she shrieked.

The man was looking cross now, his arms folded, and Dora could see Inanna opening her mouth to scream. Quick as she could, she cast a small immobility spell. Inanna was frozen with her mouth open like a goldfish.

The man stared at her for a moment, but then the box lurched, and stopped juddering, and the doors opened.

"Kids, eh?" he said to the Druid, eyebrows raised, and the Druid managed a wan smile.

Dora released Inanna and they stumbled out of the lift in relief.

"I'm sorry," said Dora. "It's just – I didn't want –"

To her surprise, Inanna grinned at her. "It's all right," she said. "It's a good thing you stopped me. When I scream, it's very, very loud."

"I can imagine," said the Druid, dryly.

The moving box had brought them close to the way out. They could see, just across a large open space, several glass doors swishing open and shut as people walked through them and, beyond them, daylight.

"At last!" said Jem, and started pushing the Druid towards the doors.

But just as they got close, an angry voice shouted from behind them. "Oy, you kids! Where are you going with that wheelchair? That's hospital property!"

A man in green overalls was gesturing at them and walking very fast across the entrance hallway. A few people had turned at the sound of his voice, and now another man in green was heading over.

"Run!" said Jem, and they broke into a trot, heading for the doors. The wheelchair was hard to manoeuvre at speed and it kept slewing from one side to the other, scattering a few people that were close by, but they made it out before the men reached the doors and then Dora, quickly throwing a spell behind her as they ran, managed to immobilise most of St Thomas's outpatient department.

"Quick!" she gasped. "It won't last long – too many people!"

They hurried to the busy road in front of them just as a large red bus drove past.

"We want that bus – it goes to Waterloo Station," said the Druid through gritted teeth, his knuckles white on the arm of the wheelchair as Jem slung it round and headed towards the place where the bus had stopped.

They clambered in, a friendly man in the front seat helping them stow the Druid in the disabled section. Dora peered back at the hospital entrance. Her spell had worn off and the two men in green were on their way towards the road, looking around everywhere for the wheelchair.

"Tickets? Oyster card?" said the bus driver.

The men had spotted the bus and were running towards it.

The Druid, after a glance out of the window, fished the railway ticket out of his coat pocket with a wince. He passed his hand across it, murmuring a few words under his breath, and gave it to Inanna, who was closest. She held it out to the driver with her haughtiest expression.

Dora held her breath, but the driver, after a moment's hesitation, nodded. The doors closed and the bus juddered then roared off, just as the men in green panted up to it. Dora collapsed into the plush seat next to Jem. They had done it. They had escaped!

The bus lurched through bustling London traffic, taxis beeping and motorbikes and bicycles weaving in and out around it.

"It's horribly noisy," Dora said, peering out of the grimy window. "I'd much rather be in a cart."

"What? With sheep eating your hair?" said Jem, whose eyes were sparkling. "This is *much* more fun. Look, Dora – no horses, no ruts in the road, and we're going along at a gallop!"

They were moving quite fast, Dora thought, but she found the sheer numbers of people and vehicles all around them completely bewildering.

She glanced at Inanna, sitting by the Druid's wheelchair. She seemed quite at home in the bustle.

"It's not too different from Ur-Akkad," said Inanna, seeing Dora's look. "We have horseless carriages as well – though they're not as noisy or smelly."

"Run on extracted magic," murmured the Druid, eyes half closed. "Won't be working now we've taken the amber."

Inanna looked thoughtful. "They won't be able to control the magic-users, any more, will they?" she said. "Will the empire fall?"

"More than likely," said the Druid. "And that's no bad thing. It's been around for far too long already. Besides – if we hadn't taken the amber, Smith and Jones would have. Either way the empire was doomed. At least this way, the world it was based in might get to survive."

Inanna nodded and put her hand up to the amber. "Is this – is it mine now?"

The Druid gave her a calculating look. "I'd say it's yours to take if you can control it. But I wouldn't recommend trying that just yet. And you won't be able to take it back to Akkad. Not till we've sorted out Lord Ravenglass. You and the amber had better come to the forest with us."

He closed his eyes, wincing as the bus passed over a pothole. He looked, thought Dora, as if he might pass out again, and she wondered whether to try a spell to keep him conscious.

But just then the bus stopped, and the conductor shouted, "Waterloo Station!"

"Our stop," said the Druid. Jem grabbed hold of the handles of the wheelchair and, with a bit of help from Dora and Inanna, managed to get him off the bus in one piece.

"Right," Jem said, looking round for directions. "What train did you say we need to take?"

Chapter Twenty-two

Cat and Simon's house had the curtains drawn and looked deserted. Inanna pushed the Druid up the path and Dora banged loudly on the knocker, but there was no answer. Jem slipped round the side of the house and then returned a few minutes later, beckoning them.

"There's a door open round the back!" he said. "Come on!"

They squeezed down the narrow side passage, the Druid's wheelchair snagging on stray plant pots and bits of abandoned bicycles, and entered the back garden. Jem was right – the kitchen door was unlocked, and after calling out a few times to check if there was anyone in the house, they carefully pushed the Druid into the kitchen and followed behind.

"What day is it?" said the Druid, frowning.

Jem shrugged. "I've got no idea. Is it the same as our world?"

"It should be," said the Druid, trying to think. "What day was it when I left?"

"Market day," said Dora. "Jem and I got to Akkadia the next morning."

"We entered the labyrinth on the day of the moon," said Inanna. "And left it that evening."

The Druid grimaced. "I *think* that means it's Thursday here. So they'll be at school. We'll have to wait till four o'clock."

"Well, if we have to wait," said Jem, "I'm having something to eat. I'm *starving!*"

Dora grinned at him. She felt hugely relieved that they had escaped the hospital and were somewhere that was quiet and safe. She was also looking forward to seeing Cat and Simon again. The kitchen of their house felt warm, cosy and familiar. And from what she remembered from last time, the food they had here was rather impressive.

Jem was already raiding the cupboards, opening packets and boxes and trying their contents. After a few unlucky choices, which made him screw his face up, he managed to gather a selection of flat hard cakes and sweet sticky things as well as some more familiar food like nuts and fruit and bread.

"Tuck in!" he said, indicating the feast. Inanna brightened at the sight of recognisable food, and filled a plate with fruit and nuts. Dora, after hesitating a moment, sat down and reached for some biscuits.

"I'm sure Simon wouldn't mind," she said. "It's an emergency, after all."

The Druid pulled himself up out of the wheelchair and held on to the edge of the table for a moment.

"You know," he said. "I think I can probably find my way to the front room. I need to lie down for a while."

Jem jumped up and offered him his shoulder to lean on, and together they made a tottering kind of progress towards the living room. The Druid lay down on the sofa with a sigh, and waved his hand at Jem.

"Thanks," he said. "You go and eat. Wake me at four o'clock, when Cat and Simon get back."

In the event, the Druid got woken long before four o'clock. Dora and Jem had been making a valiant effort at reproducing the drink called 'tea', which they remembered enjoying last time they were in Cat and Simon's world, and Inanna had been watching the process with amusement. But just as the kettle started to shoot steam out of its nose, they were all startled to hear the front door open. They barely had time to look for a place to hide before Florence, loaded with bags of shopping, pushed her way into the kitchen and stared at them in shock.

"What – what the – who on earth are you? What are you doing in my kitchen?"

Inanna drew herself up to her full height. "I am Princess Inanna, priestess-daughter of the ninety-ninth Sargon, ruler of Akkad and High Lord of the Universe. Who are you?"

Florence's eyes widened. "You're *what*?" she said.

Jem held up his hands apologetically. "Ignore her," he said. "She's – er – a bit mad. We're friends of Cat and Simon. We're sorry – please forgive us for being in your house! We… well, we needed to see them. And your back door was open, so…"

Florence's gaze took in the food on the table, and then she noticed the wheelchair. She frowned.

"Cat and Simon are on a school trip," she said. "But what in the world is a *wheelchair* doing in my kitchen?"

"It's mine," came a voice from behind her. She turned, and her face went white. Standing in the doorway, looking rather grey and drawn, was the Druid.

"Lou!" she said, her hand flying to her mouth. "*Lou!* But... what are you doing here? What's going on?"

"I'm sorry," said the Druid. "I tried not to... We were hoping to be gone before you got back."

"I had the afternoon off," said Florence automatically. She didn't seem to be paying much attention to what she was saying – her eyes were on the Druid, as if she couldn't believe he was there, standing in front of her, in her kitchen.

"Umm... can we get you a cup of tea?" said Jem brightly. "We think we've worked out how to do it."

Florence looked at him, and her eyes seemed to refocus. She glanced at Dora, and then Inanna, and she started to laugh a little hysterically. She shook her head in wonder at them all and then smiled at Jem.

"You know what?" she said. "A cup of tea would be just the thing."

She turned to the Druid and took in his bandaged head and the sling. "You'd better sit down," she said, and gestured at the table.

Grimacing slightly, the Druid eased himself onto a chair and then nodded at Jem.

"Tea," he said. "Please."

Florence took a gulp of her tea and made a slight face. "Not too bad for a first attempt," she said, and then gave them all a stern look.

"Right," she said. "Explanations, please."

"Well," said Jem promptly, having had time to think about it. "Me and Dora, we're friends of Cat and Simon. We go to the same... er... school. We've met their dad's cousin here before, and then we found him yesterday after he'd been stabbed – we don't know who did it – but we got him to a hospital and then when they let us out, we couldn't think where to come, so –"

The Druid held up his hand. "It's all right, Jem. Florence knows about the kingdom. You can tell her the truth."

Dora looked at Florence in shock. She *knew*?

Cat and Simon's mother knew all about the kingdom?

"But – but how come you never told Cat and Simon?" she blurted out. "They didn't know *anything* when we met them!"

It was Florence's turn to look shocked. "Cat and Simon *know* about the kingdom? You mean you really *are* friends with them? When did this happen?" She turned to the Druid, her expression furious. "You *promised*! You agreed you would leave them alone!"

He looked stricken. "I'm sorry, Florence. I tried. Really I did. But it turns out Mother was an heir – she had a piece of deep amber. When she died it got left in this house. I had no idea you'd all move here! And then Simon activated it by accident… I kept away until the last minute!"

"Yes, he did," said Jem, and, ignoring the Druid's increasingly frantic gestures to shut up, continued cheerfully: "He didn't get here till it was nearly all over. We could have done with him earlier, I can tell you! But Simon did a great job with the sword, and Cat was brilliant! She took the amber and then she banished Smith and Jones – and Lord Ravenglass too!"

The Druid slumped into his chair and raised his eyes to heaven. Then he looked apprehensively at Florence. She was frowning in disbelief.

"The amber? A piece of deep amber? And... Lord Ravenglass? Cat *banished* Lord Ravenglass? And this was all – what – last week? After they found the sword?"

She turned to the Druid. "A rift must have opened," she said. "That's why the sword appeared, isn't it? Gwyn *did* give it to you!"

The Druid nodded. "I'm sorry," he said again. "But it's rather out of our hands now. Ravenglass is after all the pieces of amber – he wants to remake the crown. We're not exactly sure why, but we think Lukos might be involved."

Florence closed her eyes and kept them closed for what seemed a rather long time. Then she took a deep breath and opened them. She surveyed them all with a resigned expression. "So. It's come to that. Not much chance of keeping them out of it, then, after all."

She turned to the Druid. "I'm sorry," she said sadly. "For sending you away. Maybe you were right. It was foolish trying to protect them from... all that. I just wanted them to have a *normal* life. Nothing dangerous. Nothing dark. And you – you just couldn't *do* ordinary. Magic clung to you like it was part of your skin, all the time. I couldn't keep them from it with you here… Maybe I shouldn't even have tried."

The Druid reached out his good hand and brushed a tear away from her cheek with his thumb. She sniffed and tried to smile, and the Druid grinned back. He looked, thought Dora, as if he'd won a bag of gold at the Autumn Joust.

"So," said Jem. "Where *are* Cat and Simon? Did you say they were on a school trip?"

Florence frowned and looked as if she were trying to work something out. Then her face cleared and she slammed her hand down on the table with a cry.

"Caractacus!" she said. "That blasted creature! He was here! He put a spell on me – I've only just realised! Cat and Simon went with him. They must be in the kingdom!"

"He'll have taken them to the forest," said the Druid. "For safe-keeping. Which is where we need to go, too. But without Cat and the amber, I'm not sure how we're going to get there."

Inanna coughed, and gestured at the amber jewel round her neck. "We have mine," she said grandly. "You'll just have to teach me how to use it!"

Chapter Twenty-three

Inanna was standing in the middle of the kitchen, holding the amber out in front of her and saying, in a very cross voice, "I *command* you to obey me!"

Dora was fighting the urge to giggle. It wasn't funny, really. They needed Inanna to get some kind of control of the amber or they would be stuck in Simon and Cat's world till the Druid recovered his strength, or someone thought to come and rescue them. But the sight of Inanna's haughty expression as she tried to bend the amber to her will, and the way the Druid was trying his best to be patient while obviously wanting to strangle Inanna with one of her jewelled braids, was making it increasingly hard for Dora to keep a straight face. And then when Inanna finally managed to get the amber to do something, it produced not the goblet of wine it was asked for, but a rather startled-looking goat, which looked all round the kitchen in astonishment.

After a weary gesture from the Druid, it disappeared with a plaintive 'Meh-h-h'. Dora wanted to lie down on the floor and cry with laughter. She didn't dare catch Jem's eye.

"All right. Enough for now," said the Druid. "You've made it do something, at least. We'll have a break and try again later."

"Maybe some food?" suggested Florence. She pulled a saucepan out from one of the cupboards and filled it with water. As she put it on the cooker, there was a loud banging at the door. They all froze.

"Is it – could it be Smith and Jones?" whispered Dora, her eyes wide. "Could they have found us already?"

The Druid was concentrating intently, as if he was trying to feel for the presence of the two crow men. Dora's insides flipped as there was another loud bang at the door. She started to gather her magic, but she knew she was no match for them both, and unless Inanna managed something miraculous with the amber, they were trapped.

The Druid, noticing her white face, patted her on the shoulder. "The house is warded," he whispered. "Mother set the spells, and Albert renewed them last week. They won't be able to bring their full power in here. But anyway, I don't think it's them…" He put his head on one side, as if listening hard, and then a broad grin lit up his face.

"It's Albert!" he said. "And I do believe Mother is with him!"

At that moment there was an almighty crash at the door and almost instantly it flew open. Cat and Simon tumbled in, wearing a rather strange assortment of kingdom finery, followed by Albert Jemmet, holding two motorcycle helmets. Behind him came the silvery figure of Great-Aunt Irene.

"Mum!" shouted Cat, and ran into the kitchen with Simon right behind her. She gave her mum an enormous hug, and then looked round the room in astonishment. "Uncle Lou! Dora! Jem! And…?"

"Princess Inanna," said Jem, bowing to Cat and giving Simon a grin. "We rescued her. It's a long story."

"Simon!" said Florence, as she wrapped him

up in a tight embrace. "Cat! You're all right. You're both all right. Thank goodness!"

The introductions and the swapping of stories took a very long time. Florence made vast quantities of pasta and Albert kept everyone supplied with drinks and eventually, despite the many questions and interruptions and retellings, they managed to piece together the events of the last few days. Jem had them all spellbound at the tale of his and Dora's adventures in Ur-Akkad, and everyone was in fits of laughter at their daring escape from St Thomas's Hospital with an Akkadian princess and the wheelchair-bound Druid. But when Simon and Cat started to explain their encounter with the man in the ice cave, and then their trip to the palace, the laughter died. Florence got up and walked round to their side of the table, and held them both very close.

"Oh dear," she said. "Oh Simon, Cat – I'm so sorry. If only I'd been there…"

"It's all right," said Simon slowly. "Honest. I– I'm glad in a way. I know what we're fighting against now… And it's funny, but it's made Dad more real, somehow. I know where he came from, what he stood for."

There was a pause, and then Albert took a slurp of tea and looked round at everyone.

"It seems to me we have plans to make," he said. "In the forest we have had a suspicion for a while that Lukos might be involved in this whole business – but now we *know* that he is. Which means there's only one reason Ravenglass wants the Amber Crown."

"He means to release him," said Great-Aunt Irene, as if she could hardly believe it. "Release the Lord of Wolves."

"Just so," said Albert. "And it's up to us to stop him. We can stay here for now – even if Ravenglass finds out where we are, we have two pieces of amber. He won't dare come against us directly. But we're down one of our number." He nodded at the Druid's sling and rather rakish head bandage. "And there's still one piece to find."

"I'm not done for yet, Albert," said the Druid. "A good night's rest…"

Albert shook his head firmly. "You'll be no good to anyone for a few days at least," he said. "You look like one of the walking dead."

Great-Aunt Irene coughed, pointedly.

"Er… well… Apologies for my turn of phrase, Irene," Albert said, with a bow in her direction. "But you have to admit, he looks more of a ghost than you do."

The old lady put her head on one side and contemplated the Druid fondly. "Louis, my dear. You do look rather… under the weather. On the other hand," she glanced across at Florence, "you also seem happier than I've seen you in years. *So* glad you two seem to have made it up!"

Cat looked at her mum. Florence had gone rather pink.

"Well, well," said Albert, catching their glances. "Always nice to see old friends reconciled. But we need to make plans."

"Indeed," said the Druid with a cough, looking faintly uncomfortable. "Plans. Good idea, Albert. And stop looking at me like that, Mother! Or I'll make you go back in that locket!"

Great-Aunt Irene gave him a benevolent smile and then turned to Cat. "He was so upset when they fell out, you know. So nice to see them friends again!" she said in a stage whisper.

But just at that moment there was a tremendous bang – and on the table in front of them nine silver goblets appeared next to a large jug of Sumerian wine.

Inanna clapped her hands in delight.

"I did it!" she said. "I've mastered the amber!"

Florence insisted on substituting apple juice for wine in the children's goblets.

"If it's anything like I remember from last time you visited Ur-Akkad, Lou, it's definitely not for children," she said firmly.

They had just raised their glasses for a toast, to Inanna and the fire amber, when there was another loud bang – this time at the front door.

Florence pushed her chair back and cautiously headed up the hallway.

"Who is it?" she called as she reached the door. The answer was muffled, but it seemed to satisfy her, because she opened the door and let the visitor in.

Cat took one look at the tall, good-looking man standing in the kitchen doorway and immediately wished she'd had time to change out of her rather grubby kingdom tunic.

"Sir Bedwyr!" cried Dora. "How did you get here?"

The knight bowed and blew a kiss at Cat, with a smile that made her blush.

"I was transported here by the magicks of the forest," he said. "They sent me with a message for Albert."

He looked around the kitchen, spotted the Druid, and saluted.

"Well met! It seems my message may be of importance to all of you. The forest has found the whereabouts of the final piece of amber, the sea amber. Fittingly enough, it's on a ship, and at the moment, that ship is sailing the Adamantine Sea."

It was nearly midnight before Cat, Simon, Dora and Jem got off to bed. Inanna had retired much earlier, claiming the effort of working the amber had left her utterly exhausted. She'd half fallen asleep on Jem's shoulder and then insisted that he help her upstairs. Cat, seeing Dora's expression and Jem's hesitation, had taken Inanna in hand herself, ushering her up to her bedroom and finding her a clean pair of pyjamas. Now, finally, the others had decided to give up as well and say their sleepy goodnights.

Florence was asleep on the sofa, and Sir Bedwyr was snoring in an armchair, but the Druid and Albert were still up, pouring over a set of old almanacs and maps Sir Bedwyr had brought with him, trying to pinpoint the current whereabouts of the Adamantine Sea. Apparently it moved between worlds. It had a predictable cycle but it required several complex calculations to pin down, and neither of them was in the best shape for getting those calculations right. As Cat left the room, she could hear Great-Aunt Irene snorting in exasperation and pointing out to the Druid that he had divided thirty by three and got twelve – again! She smiled and closed the door gently. They would work it out eventually, she was sure – and then they could use her jewel to travel there and snatch the sea amber before Lord Ravenglass could get his hands on it.

She yawned. Inanna was fast asleep, so Cat pulled out a mattress and some spare blankets from under her bed for her and Dora to sleep on. She couldn't be bothered to get undressed. She'd worry about clean clothes in the morning. She wrapped herself in a blanket and, as Dora settled down next to her, Cat gave her a sleepy grin.

"It's really nice to see you again," she said. "We've done all right, haven't we, between us? I've got the earth amber and Inanna's got the dragon amber. The queen still has the sky amber, and we've almost got the sea amber. Lord Ravenglass will be *furious*."

Dora's eyes were almost closed, but she nodded sleepily.

"Mmm…" she said. She smiled. She felt warm, safe and very hopeful now that they would find the last piece of amber.

Next door, Jem was already snoring, but Simon was still awake. He had released the little furry creature, Frizzle, from his cage and given him a few choice bits of carrot to nibble. Frizzle had chirruped and bounced up and down, flapping his stubby wings and purring madly. Now he was snuggled up in the crook of Simon's neck, and Simon was lying, unable to sleep, staring at the ceiling. He tickled Frizzle absently and the little creature purred. Simon was thinking about Lukos, the Lord of Wolves.

He had no idea what he really looked like. All he could see when he closed his eyes was a gaunt pale face with startling blue eyes. The face of his father. The image burned into Simon's mind as he drifted uneasily off to sleep.

Epilogue:
The Kingdom

Lord Ravenglass was not, in fact, furious. He was, on the contrary, feeling rather pleased with himself. Smith and Jones had returned, and they had good news.

"It's on a ship," said Mr Smith, with an eager expression. "In the Adamantine Sea."

"And do we know where that is, just now?" asked Lord Ravenglass, twirling one of his dark ringlets as he contemplated his accomplices.

"We are close to completing the calculations," said Mr Jones, in his dusty voice. "We thought it best to let you know immediately."

"You did well," said Lord Ravenglass graciously. "I commend your dedication. Get the calculations finished with all speed – and *get* there, before the forest sends an agent."

The two men bowed low and backed out of his chambers. As they did so, they seemed to shimmer and then disappear. Lord Ravenglass smiled. He couldn't resist a few little steps of a jig. Then he reached for a pastry from a nearby bowl and popped it into his mouth. He chewed happily and then wiped a few crumbs from his moustache with a lace handkerchief.

"Excellent," he murmured to himself. "Excellent."

He strode through the palace, blasting a few servants out of the way with well-aimed hexes, just for the fun of it. It wasn't long before he reached the depths of the palace cellars. He halted in front of the blue light of the ice cave.

"Lukos! I have news!" he called out. "We've found the last piece!"

From the ice, a man emerged. He was gaunt and pale, and his eyes were blue, but there the resemblance to Gwyn Arnold ended. His expression was mad, and a little bit dangerous, and there was cruelty in his thin lips as they twisted into a smile.

"Did the children escape?"

Lord Ravenglass waved his jewelled hand airily. "Of course. They took the amber with them and returned to their own world. You were right – the boy knew. He had broken the enchantment. It's no matter – I put a concealed spell on him before he went back to his chambers. When they are all gathered, when they have both bits of amber in the same room, the spell will be activated. Then we just have to wait till he falls asleep for it to properly wrap him up in its power." Lord Ravenglass snapped his fingers. "He'll return to us like a lost lamb to the fold."

Lukos nodded and bared his teeth in an almost snarl. "And *then*, brother, then we will be ready to remake the crown – and destroy the worlds."

ABOUT THE AUTHOR

C. J Busby grew up living on boats with her family and spent most of her childhood with her nose in a book – even when walking along the road. Luckily she survived to grow up, but she still carried on reading whenever she could. After studying social anthropology at university, she lived in a South Indian fishing village and did research for her PhD. She currently lives in Devon with her three children, and borrows their books whenever they let her.

To find out more, please visit:
www.cjbusby.co.uk

THE AMBER CROWN

Don't miss Jem, Dora, Simon and Cat's

final adventure together in . . .

THE AMBER CROWN

by C.J. Busby

Out March 2015

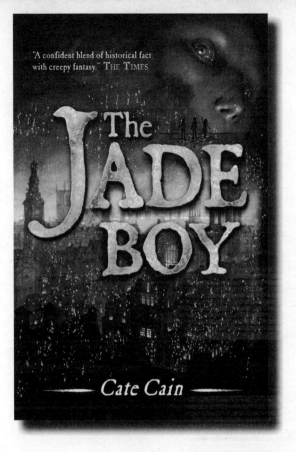

WHAT IF THE GREAT FIRE OF LONDON WASN'T AN ACCIDENT?

Sinister Count Cazalon is hatching a dark plot
for the city of London, and Jem, a twelve-year-old servant,
is at the heart of it ... How can Jem compete against
the count's powerful magic?